ELEKTRA'S
Adventures
in
TRAGEDY

DOUGLAS REES

RP|TEENS
PHILADELPHIA

~For JO~

Copyright © 2018 by Douglas Rees

Hachette Book Group supports the right to free expression and the value of copyright. The purpose of copyright is to encourage writers and artists to produce the creative works that enrich our culture.

The scanning, uploading, and distribution of this book without permission is a theft of the author's intellectual property. If you would like permission to use material from the book (other than for review purposes), please contact permissions@hbgusa.com. Thank you for your support of the author's rights.

Running Press Teens
Hachette Book Group
1290 Avenue of the Americas, New York, NY 10104
www.runningpress.com/rpkids
@RP_Kids

Printed in the United States of America

First Edition: May 2018

Published by Running Press Teens, an imprint of Perseus Books, LLC, a subsidiary of Hachette Book Group, Inc.
The Running Press Teens name and logo is a trademark of the Hachette Book Group.

The Hachette Speakers Bureau provides a wide range of authors for speaking events. To find out more, go to www.hachettespeakersbureau.com or call (866) 376-6591.

The publisher is not responsible for websites (or their content) that are not owned by the publisher.

Front cover images: Young Woman © Getty Images/wundervisuals; Highway © Getty Images/duha127

Print book cover and interior design by T. L. Bonaddio

Library of Congress Control Number: 2017939858

ISBNs: 978-0-7624-6303-9 (hardcover), 978-0-7624-6304-6 (ebook)

Printer LSC-C

10 9 8 7 6 5 4 3 2 1

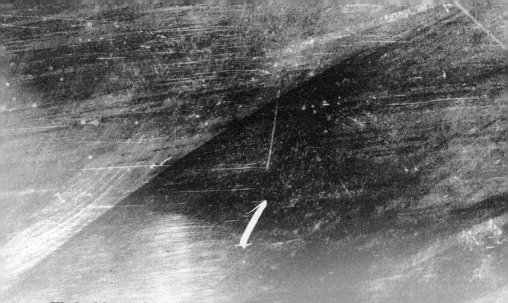

1

We had been driving for four days when I decided to kill
my mother. I had been considering it ever since we left
Mississippi, and when I saw Guadalupe Slough for the first
time, the only thing restraining me was that Thalia, my kid
sister, was in the back seat. I'd have had to kill her, too.
And Thalia wasn't guilty of anything worse than trying to
be cheerful.

But Guadalupe Slough overcame even her powers
of denial.

"Oh my God," Thalia said. "Where are we, Mama?"

It had been a long haul from Mississippi, with a lot
of night driving, and a lot of fighting between Mama and
me. Thalia had basically kept her mouth shut. Poor kid—
wedged into the back seat of Mama's ancient Volkswagen bug, Thalia hadn't made much more noise than the

cardboard boxes and paper bags that filled the rest of the space. Less, actually. The boxes rattled.

But Mama and I had managed to fill the two thousand miles' worth of silence with conversation. Pretty much the same conversation. It went something like this:

ME: Mama, this is crazy. Running away to California is not the answer. And besides, I'm sixteen. That's old enough to decide who I want to stay with, and I want to stay with Daddy. Turn around and take me home.

MAMA: Elektra, I'm sorry you can't appreciate what I'm doing for you. I'm sorry you can't appreciate what an adventure this is, and I'm desperately sorry that you can't appreciate the favor I'm doing in rescuing you from Mississippi. But whether you can appreciate any of those things or not, they're part of your life now, and you're going to have to accept them even if you don't want them. Trust me, in a year, you're going to thank me.

ME: I will never thank you for taking me away from everything I've ever known.

MAMA: That's part of the trouble: Mississippi *is* all you've ever known.

ME: Mississippi has everything that makes life worth living for me.

MAMA: You, young woman, were turning into a Southern

belle. And I will not have a daughter of mine go down that road.

ME: I was not. And there's nothing wrong with being a belle. I want to go back home.

MAMA: No.

That was pretty much the essence of it, from the time we left home, all the way across Louisiana and into East Texas. By the time we got to West Texas, the conversation had been edited down a bit.

ME: Mama, this is kidnapping.

MAMA: You wish, Elektra.

ME: I want to go home. Take me back to Daddy now.

MAMA: I've already explained to you about five hundred times why that isn't going to happen.

ME: You haven't explained anything to me once. All you do is keep repeating that it is happening. And I want to know why.

MAMA: I've explained it.

ME: No you haven't.

By the time we were crossing Arizona, our discussion had been refined further.

ME: Mama, I want to go home now.

MAMA: Elektra, I don't give a damn what you want.

ME: That is so obvious.

And when we started the long, long drive north from Los Angeles, which was choked by traffic and smog, we had developed a sort of spoken shorthand.

ME: Mama—

MAMA: Shut up.

All the while, Thalia in the back never said anything but an occasional "Look at that."

She said it when we crossed Lake Pontchartrain, which was so big that when you were in the middle of the causeway, you couldn't see the shore you'd come from or the shore you were going to. (Which, now that I think of it, summed up our situation perfectly.) She said it when we got lost in San Antonio and drove past the Alamo while trying to find our way back to Interstate 10. (It takes a kind of talent to lose an entire transcontinental highway. My mother has this talent.) She said it when we saw our first mesa in New Mexico, our first saguaro cactus in Arizona, and our first Joshua tree in the California desert.

Mama and I both knew why she was doing it; she was trying to make this trip seem like the adventure Mama wanted it to be. My poor baby sister was afflicted with the desire to make everything better, always. She had been trying to accomplish this transformation of life for her entire thirteen years. This would have been less of an impossibility for her if she had not been born into our family. My father is Nikos Kamenides, one of the greatest scholars of ancient Greek tragedy in the country. His wife, our mama, Helen, was an unpublished poet and novelist. I was a sixteen-year-old girl in a very bad mood. For all of us, life was tragedy. And right now we were living it out in a higher gear than usual.

I knew why Mama had left Daddy: because Daddy wouldn't leave Mississippi. He was the most outstanding scholar Cleburne College had, and they all knew it. He got privilege and respect like nobody else on campus. He could have gone to a bigger, more famous school, but there he would have been with a lot of other high-powered types like himself. At Cleburne, he was unique.

Mama wanted to be unique, too, but as the years went by and nothing happened with her writing, she started to blame it on Mississippi.

"I'll never make it here," she'd complain. "I need to dwell in possibility. I need New York, or California. Hell, I need Minneapolis. Any place with people who are serious about writing. Hell, serious about anything worth being serious about. Painting, music, dance, for God's sake. This place is going to kill me."

"Emily Dickinson, whom you just abused by twisting her words, dwelled in possibility in the same house in the same town her whole life," Daddy would respond. "So can you, if you want to. We're staying."

And this became the theme of my parents' marriage—a theme they expanded on until, like the Curse of the House of Atreus, it touched everything outside itself and poisoned it. The Curse of the House of Kamenides.

My parents weren't from Mississippi the way Thalia and I were. Daddy was from Toronto. Mama came from Seattle. Daddy loved Cleburne, Toronto, and Greece. Mama felt trapped in a foreign country, she said. She also said things like, "General Sherman should have done a better job on this place"—though she said that mostly just to us.

So things had gone on that way until last year, when Daddy had taken us all to Greece for his sabbatical. After we came back from that, life was different, and worse. Each of our parents seemed to be keeping secrets from the other, and from us. After a few months, they started marriage counseling, but it didn't seem help. The "D" word hung unspoken over everything.

Then one day some slightly mysterious deal came into the plot; Mama and Daddy were "probably going to separate," and Mama would be leaving if that happened. They didn't tell us any more than that.

I decided that, if it came to a split, I was staying. Why would I do anything else? I loved Daddy more than Mama, and I loved Mississippi. Even though things at home were bad, I loved my life. I had made my decision, whatever Mama and Daddy might do.

So why did I get in the car in the first place? Because I'd had no idea that my parents were going to tell me to do it until they did it. Until they summoned Thalia and me into the living room and told us, as though they'd rehearsed the lines, that Mama was leaving, and we were going with her, right then.

Their voices were low and calm and the air in the room felt ready to explode.

Thalia didn't say anything. She only gulped.

"Noooo," I said, "I'm staying here. With you."

"No, Elektra," Daddy said. "You are not. Please do as your mother and I say."

When Daddy said that, I didn't know what else to do but pack and get into the car, crying, while Daddy stood in the driveway looking sad and shouting that he loved us. Then he turned away so we wouldn't see his tears.

So, here we were, like three Trojan women, on our way to a foreign land we knew nothing about. I had not asked for this, and I hated Mama for doing it to me. I did not want to dwell in possibility. I wanted what I had. I wanted our big brick house on the edge of town, where deer came up to the windows at breakfast and the low, green hills were covered with trees and the trees wore Spanish moss. I wanted my friends, Tracy, Shawna, and Iris. I wanted my sense of myself as a part of Cleburne, and as the daughter of a great scholar. I couldn't accept the idea that all that had been taken from me. I would never accept it.

By the time we were in Louisiana, I was demanding to be taken home. Daddy hadn't meant what he'd said. He'd been blindsided and bullied by Mama. He'd just wanted to keep things from getting even worse than they were at that exact moment. He was probably already regretting what he'd done. Hadn't he cried?

Something weird was going on. I kept texting him and getting no answers. And when I did the same to Tracy and Shawna and Iris, letting them know what had happened to me, only Shawna responded.

GOOD LUCK GF. Can't talk now. S.

My other two best friends didn't even do that. It made no sense. None.

Still, once we were on the California coast, I began to think there was an outside chance that Mama might be onto something, even though I would never, ever, have said so aloud.

For one thing, I mean—dude—it was California. Have you ever seen a TV series about Mississippi? One that didn't feature burning crosses? And here was LA in all its crowded, smoggy promise. Melrose Avenue. Hollywood Boulevard, Topanga Canyon. We didn't see any of those things, but the big green road signs told us they were there, just beyond our sight. And the ocean, not the Caribbean Sea, but the Pacific Ocean, was on our left shoulder playing tag with the highway. Not wine-dark like the sea of Homer's epics, but gray and calm and powerful as life and death, it told us we had come as far as we were going to get. And when we saw it for the first time, and Thalia said, "Look at that," both Mama and I said, "Yeah."

And then as LA thinned out and the oak-studded mountains and blue skies appeared, the country started singing a strange new song, with words I couldn't quite hear and wouldn't have known if I had heard them. But the golden hills studded with oak trees seemed familiar somehow—they made me think of the shields of ancient Greek warriors. I wished that Daddy had been here, so I could have said that to him. He would have been proud of me.

The mood in the Volkswagen lightened slightly. Just slightly.

Then came San José. At rush hour. Highway 101, which had been a long, graceful sweep of driving ever since we'd left Ventura, turned into a parking lot. I don't mean the traffic slowed. I mean, it stopped. For more than an hour. Three lanes going north, going nowhere. There was a huge semi on one side of us and a gigantic gray SUV on the other, just right for crushing Volkswagens. Behind us was a white panel truck with a plumber's sign on the front, and ahead of us was car after car after car, none of them moving.

The Volkswagen did not have air conditioning.

The slightly lightened mood returned to its previous level.

ME: My God, how do people live like this?

MAMA:

ME: You would think that in a place like this, people would at least drive intelligently.

MAMA:

ME: Do you realize that we are absolutely trapped here? We are wide open to terrorist attack. Hell, this may be a terrorist attack, for all we know. How hard would it be to—

MAMA: Shut up or get out and walk.

ME: Walk? Walk where? I'm two thousand miles from my home.

THALIA: Look at that.

Sirens blaring, lights flashing, a pair of police cruisers slowly edged past the frozen river of metal. The shoulder gave them just enough room to get by. Behind them came a blue ambulance so huge it seemed too big to follow. But somehow it did. The cruisers and the ambulance slowly disappeared, leaving their fading howls behind to keep us company.

Then, after another hour, which felt like a week, the lane next to us began to move. Inches. And after another long time, the car in front of us moved. And we moved to where it had been. And stopped.

ME: I'm hungry.

MAMA:

THALIA: Want some crackers?

ME: No. I want dinner. It's time.

MAMA:

THALIA: There's some apples.

MAMA: When we get where we're going, we'll find a
place to eat. In the meantime—

ME: Shut up?

MAMA: Yes.

THALIA: Mama, would you like an apple?

MAMA: Thalia, shut up.

It was after seven o'clock when we finally passed
the line of wrecked cars pulled to the side and scattered
glass and car parts still blocking one lane. At last, the road
opened up.

I couldn't believe how bright it still was. Back home,
the shadows would be wrapping everything in night by now.

"I'm north," I thought. "This is the North." That shining
blue sky made me feel farther from home than ever.

Traffic was moving quickly now, and the off-ramps
ticked by. There were a lot of them. There was nothing
much to see along the highway—just a lot of treetops,
electric signs, and square buildings—but at least we were
moving. And at last we saw the sign that said GUADALUPE
SLOUGH NEXT RIGHT.

We swung off 101, looped around, and headed west
with the sun in our eyes. And before I could complain—

"Another highway? How much farther are you going to take us?"—a sign that read GUADALUPE SLOUGH, and an arrow pointing right, told me I was too late.

Mama followed the arrow, and suddenly we were in another world.

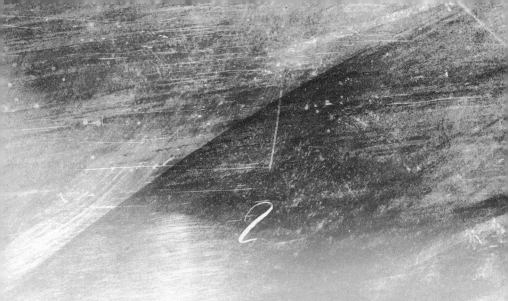

It looked like any small town might, if that small town had been built by a lost civilization of aliens equipped with a whole pile of do-it-yourself books they hadn't been able to read. They'd built everything by studying the pictures.

In some places, they had built Victorian houses, two-storied and painted white, up on mounds of earth twenty feet high. Other places, like down on the broad, silent streets, were small, square stucco houses with flat roofs and a single tall cactus growing by the door. A few resembled log cabins, including a tiny one right on Main Street that had signs that read PUBLIC LIBRARY and PAY YOUR UTIL-ITIES HERE. Next door to the library was a fire station that looked like a barn. The engine, which I could see through the station's open doors, was like something Mickey and Donald might have driven to a fire. Cute, but did it work?

On the opposite side of Main Street was a big mural portraying Aztec warriors—or maybe the aliens—in possible battle with a volcano. Below the mural was a restaurant and a sign that read EL DINER. And next to the diner stood a long, stucco building with huge snakes painted all along its roof line. The word MERCADO hung over the doors.

When we turned off the main street, I spotted a second restaurant, this one larger and painted pink with a blue electric sign that said ALIX'S. Alix's held down the southwest corner of the little town, and the freeway was not far off in that direction. We turned back around and followed the street north toward the bay. In the northwest corner of the town, we discovered a ruin of tumbled bricks that had apparently been built as a castle for birds. Anyway, every swallow in California was swooping in and out of the holes in the walls that were left standing. Continuing along the bay driving east, there was a flat, dusty path and a couple of metal picnic tables close to the edge of the water. No doubt this was what passed for a park.

Now, understand, this whole town was not more than six blocks one way and four blocks the other. Believe me when I tell you that there was no other traffic on the wide, cracked streets. Then explain to me how a woman with two master's degrees, a valid driver's license, and forty-one years of life experience can fail to find the street she is looking for.

We ground up and down and back and forth, passing the market, the fire station, the library that Daniel Boone had built with his own hands, and the big pink restaurant, so many times that we qualified as long-time residents. Thalia even stopped saying "Look at that," because we had, we had.

I tried to fill the silence by saying "restaurant" and "diner" every time we passed either one. But Mama, who had apparently decided to starve us to death to save money, ignored my attempts to be helpful.

Then, somehow, we turned a corner and found ourselves on Bodega Street, which was where we had wanted to be all along, and, was, of course, where we had been a few times already. It was the street that ran along the edge of the bay from the pile of bricks and swallows to the picnic benches. And between these, looking sad, lost, and crazy, sat the Vista del Mar Marina.

Say "marina" and you mean "boats." Trim, beautiful white and blue sailboats with their masts crowding together making a floating forest. Say "Vista del Mar Marina" and you mean something very different.

Vista del Mar Marina was a string of derelict hulks—sailboats, cabin cruisers, fishing boats—sinking into the mud, angled one way or another, surrounded by thin green reeds. If those boats had ever sailed, they had forgotten how to long ago. Some of them had awnings or extra rooms built onto their decks, even porches, hanging over the bows or sterns or lopsidedly along the decks. Others just looked abandoned. Their owners had disappeared like the crew of the *Mary Celeste*, and they had drifted into the bay with their engines still running and food on the tables. There, they had hit the mud bank, become trapped in the muck, and died.

They all lay there like drunken friends, about twenty of them in one ragged line in the mud and the reeds. Fifty yards beyond them, the water lapped in tiny, froth-covered waves.

"This can't be it," Mama said. "This is not it."

She stopped the car and looked hard at the hand-drawn map in her hand. "Bodega Street. Vista del Mar Marina. Slip 19."

"There is nothing else on this so-called street, Mama," I said. "This is what you have brought us to."

"It can't be," Mama said again.

"Mama, look at the map," I said. "Bodega Street. That's the bay. And in between, the word 'Marina.' This. Is. It."

Mama didn't answer. She got out of the car and slammed the door. I did the same.

"Hey, damn it. Don't leave me back here," Thalia said, pushing the seat forward and herself out.

My legs were acting like origami in reverse, trying to unfold into their original shapes. My head was aching from the noise of the road and the engine. I was hungry and thirsty.

And yet, a small flame of hope kindled itself within me. Mama had purchased a boat sight unseen. These were not boats.

But this was the marina. No other place nearby that could be. Therefore, this had all been some kind of four-day nightmare and we would now start back to Mississippi and our father and our friends.

Next week, I would be back at Makar's Fine Coffees with my set—Tracy, Iris, and Shawna—sitting over our mochas and laughing at my crazy mother. Oh, yes, please.

Mama was pacing up and down slowly along the sidewalk-less street.

"We need to ask directions," she said.

"Ask who?" I said. "This whole place is deserted."

Then, I saw that it wasn't. Out of the corner of my eye, I saw a man move. He ran—crouching over, wild hair flying behind him—and hid behind one of the boats. The whole thing only lasted a second, but that was long enough to see he was carrying a rifle.

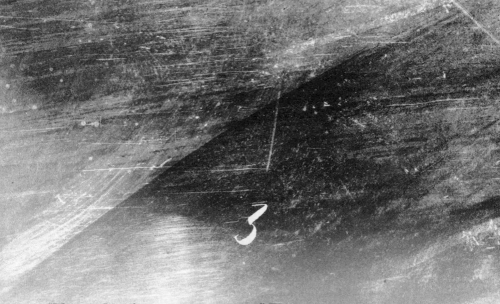

3

"Mama, there's a man with a gun," Thalia said, pointing.

But there was nothing to see now. Just the cattails waving in the wind off the sea.

"Oh, God," I said. "We're going to get murdered."

What Mama might have said or done then, I would never know, because another man appeared. He was shortish and bearded, but it looked like he had a nice face under the curly hair covering it. His glasses were round with silver metal rims. He was standing about ten feet above us on a platform that stuck out from the second story that had grown out of his boat.

It looked like it might have been a big cabin cruiser once, but the glass was missing from most of the windows and had been replaced by plywood. An old swivel chair was attached to the top of the cabin, and a low roof of corrugated fiberglass on four-by-fours covered the open stern.

Mama immediately turned to him and said, "Excuse me, please. I'm trying to find the Vista del Mar Marina. Slip 19. Can you help me?"

The man looked down at us. He seemed surprised to see us, but at least he wasn't hiding in the reeds with a rifle that was probably aimed at us at this moment. Thinking of that, I went and stood behind the Volkswagen, hoping it was bulletproof.

"The Vista del Mar Marina?" the man on the platform said. "There's no such place. Oh, no. Wait a minute. I mean, there's no such place, but you're here. That's Slip 19 right there. We're next-door neighbors. Anyway, we're going to be for the next few minutes."

I had no idea what he meant by that last statement, and I didn't care.

"Excuse me, sir, there's a man with a gun hiding behind your boat," I shouted.

"Oh. That's Ralph. He's all right. Well, he's not all right. But the gun is. It doesn't shoot. Probably not, anyway."

"How do you know it doesn't shoot?" I said.

"Because most of his don't," the man said.

I had been to enough faculty parties back home to know this man was drunk.

"Sir, my girls and I have just driven two thousand miles from Mississippi," Mama said. "We're looking for the Vista del Mar Marina, and if I understand you correctly, this is it. But there has to be a mistake. May I show you my paperwork?"

The man pulled a revolver out of his pocket and pointed it at his face. "Ralph said this one would work, but who knows? Guess I'll find out. I'm committing suicide in about twenty minutes." He tried to put the revolver back in his pocket, but that was too hard for him, so he stuffed it in his belt instead. "What the hell. I'll take a look at your paperwork. I'd love to see it."

He staggered over to the edge of the platform and looked down at a ladder that started at his feet.

"Actually, you'd better come up," he said. "I don't think I can handle those steps right now."

"If he's going to commit suicide anyway, why is he worried?" I said to Thalia in a low voice.

"Mama, don't go up there," Thalia said. "He's a crazy drunk man with a gun."

Mama stood as tall as she could and straightened her shoulders.

"Wait here," she said and climbed up the ladder. Every board in it creaked, and even in the near-dark, I could see it wobble.

"I have this ad," I heard her say. She showed the man the other side of the paper with the map on it.

He took the paper, held it up to the fading light, and read it aloud as though he were making a speech. "Live among swallows and seagulls on this secluded strip of San Francisco Bay. Forty-foot yacht converted for family living, all amenities, convenient to fast-growing San José. Shadows of Steinbeck and Jack London fall across the streets of historic Guadalupe Slough, where wind, fog, and gentle waves still speak of Old California. Slip 19, Vista del Mar Marina. Only 150,000 dollars, cash only. Don't miss this one."

The man studied the ad silently. Then he said, "You bought that place?"

"Yes," Mama said.

"Sight unseen?" the man said.

"Yes, obviously," Mama said.

"Mind if I ask why?"

The man was leaning forward. Mama took a step back.

"I needed a place for me and my girls. This ad made it

sound perfect. And the terms were good."

The man lurched forward and hugged Mama, sobbing. She pushed him away.

"Oh, lady, lady, whoever you are, thank you. Thank you. I didn't want to do it. I didn't and now—" He pulled the pistol out of his pocket and waved it wildly over his head.

Mama, Thalia, and I all screamed at once.

"Hey, Ralph, Ralph. I don't need this. It's off, buddy. I don't have to do it," the man shouted to the reeds. "Oh, bless you, lady, bless you. And bless you, too, young ladies. Oh, oh." He threw out his arms and spun around a few times. "Tell all the truth, but tell it slant," he shouted to the sky. "I did it, I did it."

"Oh, my God," I said. "He's drunk and quoting Emily Dickinson."

Mama sidled around him and started down the ladder.

"Oh, don't go that way," the man said. "Use the inside stairs. Come on." He reached out and took Mama's arm, but she shook him off.

"Stop handling me," she snapped.

"I'm sorry, I'm sorry. You're right, I'm sorry," the man said. "But you have to understand. You just saved my life. You saved my life. And you know what happens in some cultures when you save somebody's life? They owe you forever. And I owe you, lady, forever and ever. And you, too," he added, pointing to me and Thalia. "I owe all of you." He threw out his arms and faced the sun. "I'm going to dwell in possibility," he bellowed.

Mama went down the ladder.

When she got back on the ground, I saw her eyes were scared and desperate.

"Get in the car," she said.

"God, yes."

Thalia yanked open the door and got in back.

Mama turned the key. And nothing happened.

"Oh, no, no, no," Mama said.

It was just like that damn Volkswagen to carry us two thousand miles from home and then break down as soon as we really needed it. Mama kept turning and turning the key, getting more and more scared and angry.

The man on the platform noticed that we weren't moving and he disappeared. He came out a minute later on ground level and came over to us. Mama and Thalia had already rolled up the windows.

"Are you stalled?" the man said through the glass. "Let me help. It's the least I can do."

He moved to the back of the car and started trying to push. The car moved forward a few feet.

Then there was a thump from behind. I looked, and there was another man, the wild-looking one I'd seen with the rifle, and he was pushing beside the other one. The car gathered speed.

"Put it in first," one of them shouted.

Mama did, but nothing happened. Absolutely nothing.

"Again," the one called Ralph said.

And we went pushing that damn car up the length of that street until we came to the end. By that time, the two men were panting hard, especially the one who'd been drinking, and the engine was still absolutely silent.

"I believe we can say we are well and truly fucked," I said.

"I think we'd better leave it for tonight," the man with the glasses called out.

I had to admit that that made sense.

"Girls, stay behind me," Mama said. "We have to get out, but don't let that man touch you."

"As if," I said.

"Ew," Thalia added.

So we got out.

The drunk was still standing by the back of the car. The other man was nowhere around.

"I don't think it's the battery," the drunk said. "It's probably the solenoid. These things are a disgrace to electricity."

"Please leave us alone," Mama said. "Come on, girls."

We walked back the way we'd come, leaving the man standing there in the next-to-last light of day. When we reached Slip 19, Mama took a set of keys out of her pocket and said, "Let's see what we've bought."

"What *you've* bought," I said.

What she'd bought looked pretty obvious to me. There was a small barge with a wheel-less house trailer sitting on it. Behind the trailer, at the very back of the barge, was a white picket fence and a canvas awning flapping in the wind. A ladder with missing rungs led to a sort of platform on top, also roofed by a rag of canvas. For first-class passengers, no doubt. A ramp sagged between the deck and the level of the ground. I wondered how strong it was.

Mama walked up the ramp—which bounced under her, but didn't break—sighed, and opened the door.

I found a light switch, and, for a wonder, the light came on when I flicked it. It showed us a tiny living room that took up most of one end of the thing. A kitchen ran along one wall, with a refrigerator the size of a shoebox tucked under the counter and a three-burner stove right next to the sink. You could burn your elbow while you washed your dishes. A sort of dining area was across from this with room for a family of four in it, if two of them were seven years old or less. A narrow space past the kitchen held the bathroom on one side and a closet on the other. At the very end was what was probably the bedroom, but there was no bed in it. The only pieces of furniture in the whole place were the two little padded benches at the dining table, and an L-shaped sofa covered with something the color of an unripe lemon. The whole place smelled damp and musty.

"Oh. My. God."

I turned on the faucet in the kitchen sink. After a string of deep burps, water began to flow.

"Thank the Lord," Thalia said. "I need a bathroom."

She dashed into the little room with its tiny shower and turned on the light. Then she screamed.

"What is it?" I said, rushing to the doorway.

"R-roaches," she said. "Roaches or worse. Thousands."

"There is nothing worse than roaches."

Coming from Mississippi, roaches were nothing new. But I hadn't been expecting them, and certainly not in regiments.

"Mama, I want to go to a motel," I said.

"Elektra, get real," Mama said. "The car doesn't work. And if it did, we couldn't afford a motel tonight. I've got about fifty dollars."

"Fifty dollars? How will we eat?" I wailed.

"Look, we're going to unload the car. We're going to stay here tonight. We can't do anything else. There's food in the car and we'll eat that. Then, tomorrow, we'll start working things out."

"Mama, you have brought us to hell."

"Almost," Mama said. "And right now, you have no idea how close you are to making the rest of the trip. Now shut up and help."

An edge in Mama's voice said *This is it*, the edge no child ever wants to go over because you really don't know what might be on the other side. But now I had to go to the bathroom, too, and when Thalia came back, I did. I had no choice.

I didn't see any roaches. No doubt they had disappeared to plot their next action. But even though it was clean, the bathroom was a disaster: no shower curtain, the showerhead was rusty and covered with gritty-looking white stuff, and the linoleum floor was a deep orange with black scuff marks all over it. The mirror on the medicine cabinet was cracked. But, somehow, there was toilet paper. Yes, there was. The gods had decided to mock me with one small kindness.

Mama went to the bathroom next, and then we all set out for the dead Volkswagen.

By now, the sun had gone. A couple of yellow streetlights cast ugly glows a couple blocks away, and beyond them was the top of the big ALIX's sign, but here there was nothing but dark.

We walked up to the car, with me trying not to think about men with rifles hiding in the reeds, and we grabbed everything we could. After three trips, we had moved what we still owned into the trailer.

It wasn't much: our clothes, a few blankets and pillows, a box with snack food in it, Mama's laptop and printer, and one more box with our favorite books in it.

The rest was just a few odds and ends. I had left almost everything important to me at home. I hadn't been thinking clearly when I packed, so what I did have was my favorite three pairs of earrings, an ounce of expensive perfume I'd been given last Christmas, and the Greek fisherman's knife my father's grandfather had had when he came to America.

Mama carried the blankets and pillows into the bedroom. She stuffed her computer and printer into the closet and then took the box of snacks and put it on the dining table.

"Let's eat," she said.

I sat down across from her, and Thalia shoved in beside me. Mama pulled out corn chips, sodas, and some oatmeal cookies. Then she put the box aside and took our hands.

"Look, you two," she said. "This is bad. I know this is bad. This is not what I paid for, and I don't know yet what I'm going to do about it. But what you need to know is that this, right now, is the worst it's going to be. From now on, everything that happens has to be an improvement."

I took a corn chip, stuffed it into my mouth, and crunched it elaborately. Thalia took a cookie and nibbled it.

I wanted to believe Mama, but how could I? A week ago, I'd had a home, my own room, friends, and a father. Now I had nothing. Nothing but the sure knowledge that if things could get so bad so fast, they could get a lot worse.

The thin door of the trailer shook as somebody pounded on it.

"Don't answer it," I said.

But Mama got up.

"It could be that guy with the guns," Thalia said.

That made us get up and follow Mama.

Standing on the other side of the door was the drunk. He seemed a little more sober now and he carried a cluster of white boxes. A whole orchestra of wonderful smells rose from them.

"Welcome to the neighborhood, excellent ladies," the man said. "I'd like to offer you some dinner. And if there is any other help I can be, just ask. My name's Rob Schreiber, and I owe you my life."

He held the boxes out to us. Mama was just standing there, so I took them.

"Thank you, sir," I said.

"You have a charming accent," the drunk said. "Well, good night."

And he gave me a little bow.

"By the way," he said, turning away. "I'm having a party tonight to celebrate the fact that I didn't kill myself. Just a few friends. If you care to join us later, you'll be very welcome."

"Thank you," Mama said and shut the door.

"What is all that stuff?" Thalia asked.

"I don't know," I said. "But it smells like food."

And it was. Each box had something different, and everything in the boxes was strange. Bits of meat and vegetables, and some kind of soup.

"My God," Mama said. "Pâté de fois gras." She dipped her finger into the soup. "Gazpacho," she said. "Let's eat."

I started off slow on the pâté, but it was wonderful, so I tore into the rest of the boxes. We all did. In a few minutes, everything was gone.

I had never had a better meal in my life, and my mood greatly improved.

All of a sudden, Mama started to cry. Just a few tears that she wiped away as fast as they fell.

Thalia put out her hand and held Mama's.

"Well, Mama, you were right," she said. "Things are already starting to get better."

And Mama smiled. "Maybe."

"Oh, really?" I said. "Is he going to bring us breakfast, too? Breakfast in bed. Oh, wait, we don't have a bed."

"There will be breakfast," Mama said. "I don't know how, but there will be."

"Mama, why do you think that man keeps saying you saved his life?" Thalia said.

"He says you kept him from committing suicide, but what did you do?"

"All I know is I'm glad he thinks so," Mama said.

"But don't you want to ask him?"

"Not tonight," Mama said. "Maybe if we come to know him better."

"Mama, you can't mean we're going to stay here," I said.

"At this point, I don't have any idea what's going to happen," Mama said. "All we know is, we're here now."

"Are we going to the party?" Thalia asked.

Mama shook her head. "I'm too tired," she said. "And after the day we've had, I wouldn't be very good company."

"That's true enough," I said. "Besides, I don't think I want to know any more about the people in this place than I already do."

Now that we had eaten, we didn't know what to do next. The three of us sat together but alone, each feeling our weariness, while the sounds of the party next door rose.

They weren't loud noises, but Slip 19 was right next to Slip 18, and whatever they did tonight, we were going to hear some of it. The number of voices slowly grew, and music started, some old stuff with lots of brass. I thought it all sounded kind of friendly, but I wondered how we'd sleep.

Sleep. That was the next thing. We were all exhausted. When Thalia's eyes closed and her head drooped forward, Mama got up and took the blankets into where the bed belonged.

"Come help me, Elektra," she said.

Together, we folded three blankets in half and set them on the floor beside each other. Then we laid three more doubled up on top of them. That left us one more blanket and the quilt. Mama spread the quilt across two of the blankets and took the last blanket for the third.

"You and Thalia will share the quilt," she said. "I'll sleep under this one."

I had a feeling it was going to be mighty cold sleeping like this, but I knew better than to say so now.

Mama went back into the main room and woke up Thalia enough to get her over to the blankets.

"Where's the bed?" she mumbled when she saw our sleeping arrangements.

"In Mississippi," I said, handing her a pillow.

"Oh, my God," she said, but she lay down.

Mama pulled off Thalia's shoes.

"Shouldn't we get her undressed?"

"You can if you want to. I'm not waking her up again."

We both took off our shoes and our jeans and put on sweatpants. I decided to leave my shirt on for warmth and took my place beside Thalia.

Out of curiosity, I checked the time on my phone. It was almost seven thirty.

This is awful, I thought, and that was the last thing I thought for some hours.

When I woke again, Mama was breathing heavily, almost snoring, and making little puff noises as she exhaled. I felt surprisingly comfortable. I was warm enough, and the folded blankets made a pretty fair mattress.

I lay there, feeling strange and a little scared, thinking about all the things that could happen now. Would we starve? Would we end up living in a homeless shelter or under a bridge? People did, lots of them. Would we stay here, and what would that be like? Would we have money for clothes and all the extra things at school?

And why, why, why was I here at all? I'd thought I understood my parents. I was proud of them. Daddy was famous in his field, and Mama was a fine writer. I mean, she wrote fine words. Sharp and elegant. If she wasn't published, it wasn't her fault.

And sure, they had fought. We all fought, except Thalia. We were Greeks, weren't we? We had been fighting for thousands of years. When we didn't have any Trojans to fight, we'd fought the Persians, the Romans, the Turks, and the Germans. And when there was nobody else around, we'd fought each other. We were part of a great tradition but divorce was not in that tradition.

I understood some of it. Mama was frustrated as hell. It wasn't just that she wasn't published, although that was a huge part of it. It was that she couldn't handle Mississippi. She said it was rigid, hypocritical, and, worst of all, boring. She felt like she was in a magnolia cage.

I didn't know what she was talking about. I thought life in Mississippi was as rich as delta soil and as sweet as molasses. Sure there were rules, strong rules, but I knew what they were. I broke some of them and lived by others. But even the ones I broke were part of who I was, part of the place I belonged. If I couldn't live in ancient Athens, Mississippi would do.

Mama wanted something freer, and, above all, more literary. She wanted a writer's life, and she thought that was something she'd never have in Mississippi.

So maybe that explained California. But what could explain the divorce? Why would she want to leave Daddy? And for what? Pictures of a boat that wasn't even real?

And what about Thalia? Poor little cheerful Thalia always trying to make things better. What was all this doing to her? Mama was being a selfish bitch.

I reached out to touch my quietly sleeping little sister. My hand brushed over the blanket's roughness. Thalia was gone.

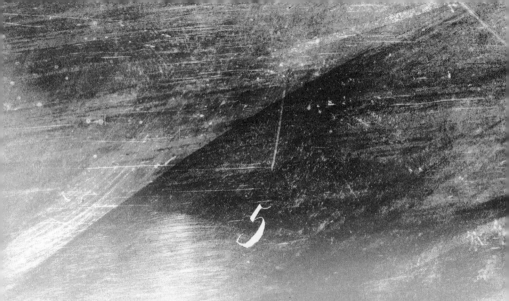

Yes, well and truly gone. No sounds came from the bath-room, no light from the front of our little abode. Gone.

"Mama, wake up. Thalia's missing."

She didn't respond, so I shook her. Good and hard.

"Whut?"

"Your daughter is missing," I said. "Get up."

Mama woke instantly. "Thalia?" she called. "Thalia?"

I got up and found the light. As I flicked it on, I heard my sister's voice thinly through the wall. Coming from next door, where all of sudden I realized the old brassy music wasn't playing.

She was singing.

"'Neath Southern stars,

In low bars,

They blew notes

High as Mars,

And they say that's

How the blues began.

The broken heart

Of some tart

Was the wail

At the start,

And they say that's

How the blues began . . ."

"What the hell?" Mama said.

"You were aware that your daughter sings," I said. "And she knows everything in Daddy's old vinyl record collection."

"Of course I know it. But what's she doing singing in the middle of the night?" Mama snapped.

We changed out of our sweatpants and tugged on our shoes. It was chillier outside than it had been before, so Mama pulled on a sweater and I grabbed a jacket, and we headed out the door.

Slip 18 was glowing, outlined in Christmas lights, and every light indoors seemed to be on as well. The party was on the platform where we'd first seen our neighbor Rob the Drunk—I was having a hard time thinking of him as Mr. Schreiber—getting ready to commit suicide.

I could see him up there now, slow dancing with an old lady who looked like she barely came up to my shoulder. They might have been doing a real dance, but I think they were just making it up as they went along. Other people were applauding and laughing, and Thalia was standing on a table singing her heart out.

Mama climbed the ladder, and I went up after her.

The party was six people: Rob and the old lady he was dancing with, another old lady, a handsome young man with olive skin and shiny black hair who looked like a Greek statue come to life, a gorgeous woman sitting next to him who was dressed like a belly dancer, and the crazy old man with the gun. Seven, if you counted Thalia.

"Hey, Rob, you got company," said the second old lady in a voice like chainsaw.

Rob spun the other old lady around so he could see who it was, and he gave us a huge smile and stopped dancing.

"Hey, everybody, it's them," he said, coming over and grabbing my hand.

"Thank you for coming. Thank you."

"Is she the one?" the belly dancer asked.

"No, that was her mom," Rob said. "But she was there when it happened."

"Thank you for keeping Rob from killing himself," the old lady he'd been dancing with said to Mama. "We'd miss him."

"Yeah, thanks," said the tall, handsome guy. "We'd miss the parties on this yacht."

"Hi, Mama," Thalia said. "I've been meeting the neighbors."

"Okay," Mama said. "That's good. Now come home. It's late."

"No, it's not," Thalia said. "It's not even midnight yet."

"Can't I get you to stay?" Rob asked. "There's some wonderful food. Wine, if you'd like it. The wine's not that wonderful, but the food's from Alix's."

"No, thank you," Mama said.

"Then before you go, can I at least explain how you saved my life?" Rob said. "These characters all know. It seems like a shame that the person who did it doesn't have a clue."

"Oh, Mama, it's such a good story," Thalia said.

Mama hesitated. I could see she didn't want to stay, but how do you tell someone, *No, I don't care how I saved your life?*

"If . . . it's important to you," she said finally.

"Great. But first let me introduce the rest of the gang," Rob said. "The tall, good-looking guy's Antonio. That's his wife, T'Pring—"

"My parents were Trekkies," the belly dancer said with a shrug.

"This lovely lady in the corner is Maizie, and the even lovelier lady who was in my arms a moment ago is Alix herself, she of the restaurant. And the wild-haired fanatic on your right is Ralph, whom you sort of met earlier."

Everyone smiled and nodded as Rob introduced them. Everyone but Ralph, who got up and went downstairs into the depths of the boat, leaving his rifle behind.

"Good evening," Mama said.

And I added, "Hi, y'all."

Thalia got down off the table and joined us.

"That was a wonderful song," Rob said. "I predict a great future for you as a chanteuse, just as soon as big band makes a comeback."

"As soon as they locate Glenn Miller," Maizie said, laughing like a dog barking.

Right on cue, the brassy old music started again. It was Glenn Miller, the big band leader who disappeared in World War II. Daddy's literary taste dates to the fifth century BC, and his musical tastes are almost as ancient.

"That's 'Moonlight Serenade,'" Thalia chirped.

Alix put her arms around Maizie and started dancing

with her. Antonio rose, bowed to T'Pring, and gently swept her into a waltz.

"Do you slow dance, ma'am?" Rob said to Mama.

"Just tell me your story, please," Mama said.

Ralph reappeared with a big jug of wine and some plastic glasses. He held them out to Mama, who shook her head, and then he turned to me.

"Yes, thanks," I said.

"No," Mama said, pushing Ralph's hand away. He filled Rob's glass and moved on.

"Well, it's like this," Rob said, toasting Mama. "I used to be a lawyer. Pretty good one. But then five years ago, I got broken open by a book. Burton Raffel's translation of *Beowulf*. Do you know it?"

"I've read *Beowulf*," Mama said.

"Me too," I said.

"It was amazing to me. The control of language. The reach across centuries to make this translation happen. The strength of the words. I cried, without knowing why. And then I found out that Raffel had been an attorney. That did it for me. I decided to abandon law and become a poet. Sold my house, sold my car, cashed out every financial I had.

"Then I moved here. I gave myself five years. It seemed

impossible. I had everything to learn about being a poet—hell, five years ago, I didn't know a pantoum from a probate—so I gave myself an incentive. If I hadn't at least started to make a career in poetry, if I hadn't sold at least one poem to a major magazine or had a paid reading—something, anything, to make me believe I was on the right course—I'd kill myself. Today was the last day of the fifth year."

"My goodness," Mama said.

"You saw what I was doing when you drove up," Rob said. "Just waiting for the last rays of sunset. And then you came up here and showed me that ad. And I knew the universe wanted me to live."

"Why?" I asked, because Rob was not making sense.

"I wrote that," Rob said. "I wrote those words. And you came all the way from Alabama—"

"Mississippi," Thalia said.

"Because of what I wrote," Rob said. "You have no idea what that means to me. I mean, in the last minutes of my earthly existence, you show up with those words in your hand—" He started to tear up and wiped his eyes with his wine-holding hand.

"Like Philoctetes the archer," Thalia said. "Justified in the sight of Zeus."

"You know *Philoctetes*?" Rob said.

"Our daddy teaches classics," Thalia said.

"Whoa. You're the daughter of *that* Kamenides? Nikos Kamenides?" Rob said.

"That's us," Thalia chirped.

Rob threw back his arms and shouted up at the clouds rushing over the moon. His wine sloshed onto my jacket. "Thank you, universe," he roared. "You like me, you like me. You really like me."

He turned to Mama. "I love your husband's stuff. Brilliant translations. And his book on Greek theater made me want to become a season ticket holder in classical Athens. If anything could make your appearance here even more magical, this would be it. Is he joining you?"

"We're divorcing," Mama said.

"They're separated," I explained.

"Oh. I'm sorry," Rob said. "I used to handle a lot of divorces. I really am sorry."

"Tell me one thing," Mama said. "Why did you write that ad?"

"J. Anthony Dumont paid me twenty-five bucks," Rob said.

"This is what he said I was buying," Mama said. Reaching into her back pocket, she pulled out two folded sheets of photographs of a beautiful sailboat in a real marina.

"Nice boat," the man said. "Wonder where it is? Oh, wait a minute. Look at that. See that way tall spire? That's the Mormon temple in the Berkeley Heights. Guess this must be the Berkeley Marina."

"So my boat is in Berkeley."

"Someone's boat is in Berkeley," Rob said. "It sure wasn't J. Anthony Dumont's."

"I need to talk to Mr. Dumont," Mama said. "Where is he?"

"My guess would be Yucatán," Rob said. "He used to talk about going there a lot. Of course, he talked a lot, period. But if you paid him a hundred and fifty thousand dollars all at once, he may have gone to the moon."

"Do you have any contact information for him?"

"No," the man said. "I mean, I have his email address, but that's it."

"So have I. It's been disconnected," Mama said.

"Uh-huh," Rob said.

"So. What I own is that thing over there," Mama said. "And you helped him sell it to me. And you lied."

"Respectfully, savior lady, I did not," Rob said. "Jack London used to be an oyster pirate on this bay. He put in at the dock here to sell his take. John Steinbeck used to come here to go fishing."

"Fishing!" Maizie cackled.

"Hush up, Maizie. There's young ladies present," Alix said.

"He used to go to Alix's to get laid," Maizie said. "Whoop!"

"At a restaurant?" I said.

"It had an upstairs," Maizie said. "Best damn upstairs on the bay. And I was the reason why."

"Maizie, I am taking you home," Alix said.

"The hell you are," Maizie said. "Get me another drink."

Ralph hurried over and refilled her glass.

"You can't have known Steinbeck," I said. "He's been dead for decades."

"Come over sometime and I'll show you my first editions," Maizie said. "Signed."

"That's enough out of you, missy," Alix said. "T'Pring, why don't you dance for us?"

"Yeah, hell. This is supposed to be a party," Maizie said.

Ralph went downstairs, or whatever downstairs is on a boat, and a minute later the music changed. Now it was Middle Eastern belly dance music. Antonio lifted his wife onto the table. Slowly and elegantly, T'Pring danced.

Now, I knew something about belly dancing. The Greeks learned it from the Turks, and it was the only thing they ever gave us to be grateful for. Mama and I had taken classes from the university extension a couple years ago. So when I tell you that I had never seen anyone dance like T'Pring before, it's not because I didn't know what I was talking about. T'Pring was not just good—she was the best. Her hands were as graceful as birds, and her hips were wicked as sin. Her feet were perfect, precise, and her spine was like no one's I'd ever seen. She moved like a snake.

Belly dancing isn't just slinging your behind around. It's a celebration of life, and that's what T'Pring was doing: celebrating Rob's life, going on from this night. I started to clap time for her. Thalia picked it up, and then Antonio, and then everybody was doing it.

Well, not everybody.

Suddenly another man arrived, waving a baseball bat and shouting. "You *culos* pipe down. People are trying to sleep."

"Hey, Mr. Gonzales." Rob smiled while T'Pring whirled on. "Thank you for coming. I've got wonderful news."

"Wonderful enough that this bat isn't going to crack your skull for you?" Mr. Gonzales asked.

"Wonderful enough that it won't hurt me if you do," Rob said. "I don't have to commit suicide."

"Now tell me the wonderful news," Mr. Gonzales said.

"Meet our new neighbors," Rob went on. "Ladies, I'd like you to meet Mr. Gregorio Gonzales. Of the Guadalupe Slough Gonzaleses. Think pilgrims of Plymouth Rock. Think first families of Virginia. Then think Gonzaleses of Guadalupe Slough. And Mr. Gonzales, these charming, wonderful ladies are the Kamenideses—Thalia, Elektra, and their mother, Helen."

"Where the hell you come from?" Mr. Gonzales asked.

"Mississippi," Mama said.

"Never heard of it," Mr. Gonzales said.

Then T'Pring was between us and Mr. Gonzales, slowly sliding a sheer black veil above her head. She draped it around Mr. Gonzales and pulled him toward her.

"Cut that out," he said, but he looked like he was fighting back a smile.

T'Pring danced him away from us, over to the corner where Alix and Maizie were.

"Well, that was unpleasant," I said.

"Mr. Gonzales doesn't like white people," Rob said. "The only way he could join us was if he came over to complain."

Mr. Gonzales had dropped the bat and was sharing a drink with Alix and Maizie.

"So why'd he come if he doesn't like white people?" Thalia asked.

"I think it's more the abstract concept of white people he doesn't like than the reality," Rob said. "Anyway, he loves to party."

T'Pring came strutting back toward us in camel walk. The music finished and a new song began, one I knew. When she started to dance again, I joined in.

I wasn't as good as T'Pring, but I know what I'm doing when the ouds and drums starting rocking the Middle East, and T'Pring laughed and started matching her steps to mine. Antonio and Rob and Thalia clapped in time with us, and Ralph slowly spun around in one spot with his arms out, something like a dervish trying to connect God to the earth, but he didn't know where to put his hands for that.

On an impulse, I moved over to him and spun, too. Then I raised my right hand over my head, reaching up to the sky, to heaven, and my left hand down toward the deck. When Ralph noticed me, he began to do the same thing. We twirled side by side until the song, a long one, ended. Then I went up on half-toe, raised both my arms over my head, and spun away from him.

Ralph went on dancing, his eyes closed, his face a mask of peace and longing.

"Go Ralph, go Ralph," Rob shouted, but T'Pring went over, took his left hand, and gently slowed Ralph down.

"I'm dizzy," Ralph told us. He sat down on the deck and said to me, "Thanks. I was wondering how to do that."

Then he lay back and put his hands behind his head.

I looked up. The clouds were almost low enough to touch, racing past me, making the moonlight flare and fade like the echoes of an old song. A moonlight serenade. All of a sudden, I missed my daddy enough to cry.

"Thanks, y'all," I said. "I'm going back to bed. Good night."

"Good night, Elektra," Mama said.

"See you soon," Thalia chirped.

"Thank you," Ralph said. "Thank you again. Don't worry about anything. I've got the first watch."

Whatever that meant. I walked across to the ladder trying to hold back my tears.

I made it back to our place without breaking down, threw myself on the floor of the bedroom, and sobbed. It hurt; it hurt so much. I hadn't ever felt anything this deep and dark before, and I cried in a way I hadn't cried since I was a little girl and our dog, Ajax, died.

A memory surfaced and wouldn't leave. I was ten years old, and I was walking with my father through my elementary school's science fair. We came to my entry, a map of the stars. I'd drawn the outlines of the Greek constellations in gold. I'd drawn the outlines of the Islamic constellations in silver, and the Mayan constellations in white. The Chinese constellations were red, and the Hindu constellations were orange. The title of my project was *Many Skies— What Do You See?* Hanging on that map was a blue ribbon.

"Who helped you?" Daddy said, putting his hands on my shoulders.

"No one," I said.

"I am in awe," Daddy said. "And right now I'm so proud, I want to raise you over my head and shout 'This is my daughter!'"

Why did I have to think about that now? Why had I let Mama drag me into the car when Daddy was in tears? He'd said go, but he hadn't meant it. He hadn't.

I pulled out my cell phone and dialed his number.

"Hi, this is the phone of Nikos Kamenides. Please leave a message after the beep."

"Daddy, it's Elektra," I managed to get out between gasps. "Please come and get me. Please, please, please."

Damn it, it was four o'clock in the morning in Mississippi. Where was he? Fast asleep, of course, with his phone silenced. But at least I'd done something. At least I'd begged. I felt a little better, and a sureness came over me that told me I was going home. Daddy would want me back. He would call, we would talk, and I would be on my way home. This would happen. The nightmare into which Mama had dragged me would end. And when I knew that, I fell fast asleep.

I woke up when Mama and Thalia came in.

"Well, those people are real nice," Thalia said.

"At least they're interesting," Mama said. "Rob knows an awful lot about literature. Of course, I don't know if he can really write."

I did not like the tone in her voice. It was the same one I'd heard come into her words when a famous writer came to Cleburne to give a reading or to meet my father. It was a tone that said, "I'm *interested.*"

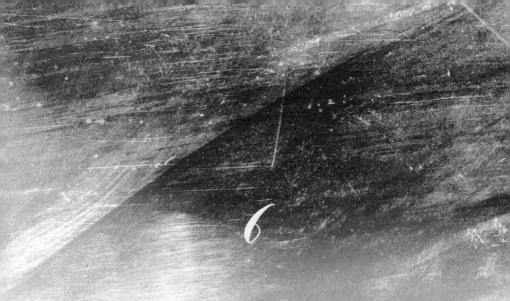

6

The next morning, I made as much noise as I could walking to the bathroom. I wanted to let the roaches know I was coming. Then I went to the front door just to see what a San Francisco Bay morning looked like.

I screamed.

The cool air or the low gray sky hadn't hauled the shriek out of me, but the large glass jar on the step at my feet had. To be more precise, the contents of the jar had. Inside was the largest, hairiest spider on the planet. This thing was so big I could see its staring black eyes. And it was trying to get out.

A scrap of notebook paper was across the top of the jar, held with a rubber band.

I slammed the door.

"What is it?" Mama said. She was up now and pulling on her jeans.

"Something disgusting from one of the neighbors," I said. "Something vile."

"Well, what?" Mama said, yanking the door open. Then she saw why I'd screamed, did the same thing, and stepped back.

"What the hell?" she said.

Thalia joined us, looking scared. Then she eased the door open a little more and said, "There's a note on the spider."

Scrawled in pencil on the piece of paper, it read:

If you have roaches put George in your place. He will take care of them. I can get another spider.

If you don't please give him back.

Ralph Cummins

"Oh, my God," I said.

"He's interesting-looking," Thalia said. "Hello, George."

"Is everything okay?" Rob said, coming out of his boat. He looked pretty hungover from the night before.

"No, it is not," I said. "We have roaches and spiders."

Rob came up onto our porch and looked at the jar.

"Actually, around here, it's roaches *or* spiders," he said. "You get yourself a tarantula and the roaches disappear. Some of them disappear inside the tarantula. The rest move on. But they keep coming back to see if he's still there, and so your tarantula stays fat and happy. Oh, wow, that's George. Ralph gave you George. Wow. He must really like you."

"What would he give us if he hated us?" I said.

"No, no. This is a huge thing," Rob said. "He loves George. Best spider he ever had."

"Do you have a tarantula, too?" Thalia asked.

"We all do," Rob said. "Ralph goes up in the hills and gets them for us. They don't like it down here. Too wet. But if you keep him inside, he'll be fine."

"But he's disgusting," I said.

"So are roaches," Rob said. "Anyway, you won't see too much of him. He's looking for breakfast, not company."

"Aren't they poisonous?" Mama said.

"Mm-hm," Rob said. "About as bad as a bee sting. But why would he bite you if you weren't bothering him?"

Because he's pure evil? I thought.

But Mama said, "Thalia, pick him up and bring him inside. We'll get used to him."

"I won't," I said.

"Hello, George," Thalia said, holding the jar up to her face.

"Since you're up, can I take you out to breakfast?" Rob asked. "The chorizo over at El Diner is to die for."

"Thank you," Mama said. "Can we do it in an hour? The girls and I need to get cleaned up."

"Just come and get me when you're ready," Rob said.

That shower. The water was hot enough, but it dribbled out with no force at all. And while I tried to scrub away the sweat and dirt of yesterday, I kept looking around for roaches. I toweled off—this was a minor triumph since there was only one towel for the three of us, and I had it first—and then I saw one of the little devils go scuttling under the edge of the toilet.

I screamed, just to protest the fact that that damned lazy, ugly spider hadn't done his job yet. Then I finished drying off and made sure to leave the towel sopping wet.

By the time the three of us were ready to stagger over next door, a soft breeze was blowing across the gray morning. We could hear a distant hiss of freeway noise, and under it, the little slaps of the waves at the edge of what I guessed was our backyard. But aside from that, everything around us was as still and quiet as it had been when we arrived. I wondered how many of those houses on the streets in front of us had anyone in them.

In the morning light, Guadalupe Slough looked even stranger than it had the night before. It did not seem to belong to any particular time. Or maybe it belonged to all the time that had ever passed there, all at once. Victorian homes, little wooden cottages, and flat-roofed stucco places, a scatter of mobile homes on weedy lots, one or two square-sided wooden towers sticking up near them, and the ruined brick building off in the distance. Above it all rose Alix's big, old-fashioned neon sign, dark now, and gray as the sky.

Thalia pranced up to Rob's door.

"We're ready, Mr. Rob," she said.

Rob came out in a T-shirt that had a picture of Shakespeare on the front and on the back said DEVISE, WIT; WRITE, PEN! FOR I AM FOR WHOLE VOLUMES IN FOLIO.—*LOVE'S LABOUR'S LOST*. On his head was a baseball cap that said I HATE BASEBALL.

"You look lovely," he said, offering Thalia his arm. But it was Mama he was looking at when he did it.

"Thank you, kind sir," Thalia said as she took it.

El Diner looked foreign, and a little sinister, with its big, scowling warriors and volcano looming over the corner where it sat.

When we went in, some tables were covered with dirty plates and at others people were finishing eating.

Everyone inside had brown skin and dark hair. One or two people waved to Rob.

It was one of those places where they make the food on grills you can see, right behind the counter. "Chorizo all around," Rob called to the cooks, of whom there were two, both of whom looked a lot like Mr. Gonzales. Then he led us to a booth. The booth was ordinary-looking except for a wooden sign on the wall above it that said CUAUHTÉMOC. The word looked like an ancient Aztec curse.

"What does that mean?" I asked.

"It's the name of the last of the Aztec kings," Rob said. "The one who led the resistance against the Spaniards. All the booths and tables are named for Mexican heroes."

I looked around and noticed a few of the others. MORELOS, HIDALGO, VILLA.

I knew who the last one was. Mama's great-great-grandfather had been in the army back in 1916 and had gone chasing Pancho Villa across Mexico after he raided Columbus, New Mexico.

"Villa wasn't much of a hero," I said. "He attacked American soil and killed a bunch of people. One of my ancestors was in the army that went after him."

"Hero," Rob said. "Hero in here, hero in Mexico. Did a

lot of good stuff from what I hear. Built a lot of schools."

I let it drop. Arguing about Mexican bandits in here might get me in trouble. Or at least served last.

A girl about my age came over with coffee and water.

"Hi, Rob," she said. "Grandpa says you're not killing yourself."

"Not for another five years, anyway," Rob said.

I had never seen people make so much fuss over a suicide that didn't happen.

The chorizo came, and it was good. It didn't look like anything special, just sausages chopped up and mixed in with scrambled eggs. But the flavor! Even in my post-party depression, it tasted wonderful.

I felt much better, and, remembering that Daddy would be calling soon and that I wasn't going to be staying here long, I allowed myself to become more curious about where I was.

"How did all the boats here end up in the mud, anyway?"

"Up until about ten years ago, that mud was part of the bay," Rob said. "Those boats were afloat. Then there was a big flood and the Guadalupe River silted up at its mouth. When the water went down, there they all were. And there they have stayed."

"Beached like the Greek ships at Troy," Mama said.

"Hey," Rob said. "That's good. Mind if I write that down?"

"Be my guest."

"Can I borrow a pen?"

Thalia had one, so Rob took it and wrote a few words on his napkin. While he wrote, he said, "The Greek ships at Troy were beached for ten years, but they were there for a reason. The Greeks were fighting a siege. We're fighting a siege, those of us who live on these boats. We're besieging life, trying to make it give us what we want. Wow. I haven't had an idea this good in weeks. Thank you."

I saw Mama duck her head and smile.

Thalia said, "Mr. Rob, do you know why Mr. Cummins was outside our place last night walking up and down with a gun?"

"He was?" Rob said. "Man, that's major. He must really, *really* like you."

"What?" Mama and I said together.

"I got up to go to the roachroom about dawn, and I saw him out there in front of our place," Thalia explained. "He'd walk about twenty steps, turn around, and walk back. Then he'd do it again. And every time he did, he'd take his rifle off his shoulder, put its butt on the ground, and then put it back up before he turned around."

"He was guarding you."

"Against what?" Thalia said.

"That varies," Rob said. "Sometimes it's the Viet Cong. Sometimes it's Mr. Gonzales. Sometimes I'm not sure who it is. All I know is, they never get past Ralph."

"He said something about taking the first watch last night," I recalled.

"He always takes the first watch," Rob said. "Walks up and down in front of his own place for a few hours most nights. But every so often, if he thinks they need it, he'll guard someone else. He guarded me once when I had the flu."

Rob wiped his mouth with his napkin. "Well, would you like anything else?"

Mama shrugged. "A job would be nice. And some immediate cash."

"What experience do you have?" Rob said.

"I taught English before I was married," Mama said. "And let's see, before that I was a dishwasher, and an inventory taker. And summers I used to pick apples on my uncle's farm. Not a long résumé."

"I'd try Alix's," Rob said.

"I'm not that kind of girl," Mama said.

"She usually needs dishwashers," Rob said. "Most of them quit. They can't handle Maizie. She's got it in for dishwashers."

"You make it sound so inviting," Mama said. "Still, I'd better get over there and check it out."

Reality was catching up to Mama this morning. I felt worried for her and Thalia, and I was grateful I wouldn't have to go through it with them. I wondered if Daddy had called back yet. I wanted to go off alone and check my phone.

Rob pulled out some money and put it on the table. His wallet was empty after he did it.

We said thank you, though Mama said it kind of softly and looked down. I think she was embarrassed about having to let Rob pick up the check.

"What are you doing with the rest of your day?" he asked.

"Unpacking, I suppose," Mama said. "Settling in."

"I'll be at the library for a while," Rob said. "It's only open noon to five on Saturday, but you should swing by."

"That little cabin place?" Thalia said. "I'll bet we've got more books in our house back home than in that little building."

"There's a good chance of that," Rob said. "But it's kind of special anyway. And there isn't that much in the slough that is. No, strike that. Not true. This slough is full of special. But the library has special all its own."

When we left the diner, the sun had turned everything yellow-gray, and I could smell the stinky salt of the bay more strongly. Up the street, some boys about Thalia's age were kicking a soccer ball and shouting to each other in a mix of English and Spanish. I noticed some brightly colored rags flapping in a front yard, little triangular flags with what I was pretty sure was Tibetan writing on them. From the house across the street came the sounds of Mexican music—lots of horns and accordions.

Rob said, "Well, good-bye. See you later," and peeled off from us.

When we got back to the barge, Daddy still hadn't called back. I helped unpack the rest of the boxes and we got our things spread around the place in about an hour.

I kept an eye out for that damn spider, but he didn't seem to be around. I kept turning, looking over my shoulder. I was sure he was lurking somewhere, waiting for a chance to stalk me. Then I had a horrible thought: we were sleeping on the floor. He could crawl right over us, and undoubtedly would.

"Come on, Daddy, call and get me out of here," I muttered.

"What?" Mama asked.

"Nothing," I said. "Listen, if you don't need me for anything, I'm going to go over to the library and check it out."

That would get me away from the spider for a little while and pass the time until Daddy called.

"Me too, me too," Thalia said.

"Sure, go ahead," Mama said. "But don't go anywhere else without me."

"Where else is there to go?" I asked, as I went out the door.

"You know what?" I told Thalia as we went down the street toward the tiny building. "If this library were in Mississippi, people would take it as proof of how backward and poor we are. But put it in California and nobody thinks a thing about it."

"You don't know what people in California think about anything," Thalia said. "Anyway, it's still a library. I like them."

"That's no distinction. You like everything," I said.

"There are things I don't like," Thalia said. "I just don't complain all the time."

Inside, the library was totally quiet, which is pretty much how you expect a library to be. But I mean, totally. I couldn't find anybody else in there except a stunning woman with golden skin and the most aristocratic nose I had ever seen. She was checking in books at the far end of the building.

The main thing I noticed, though, was the carvings. The building had almost no shelves, but it had enough carved and painted wooden sculptures to start an art museum, and they were close to life-sized. One was a mermaid, one was a bird woman with her wings folded. One was a queen or a princess, one was a witch. All of the statues had the same face.

"Can I help you?" the golden woman asked. From her tone, she was pretty clearly hoping the answer was no.

"Just looking, thanks," I said.

"We're new," Thalia said. "This is our first time here."

"I know," the golden woman said. "If you'd been here before, I'd remember you. Well, I'm Angela Torres, the library clerk. If you need a librarian, just ask over there. Otherwise, knock yourselves out. Be careful where you step. Boozer's around here somewhere."

At the words "around here somewhere," I started checking corners for another tarantula, but then I heard a long, comfortable groan. In the corner, on our right as we'd come in, was a desk and a man behind it who seemed to be asleep. But the groan hadn't come from him. Crammed into the space behind him was a dog. I could see one hind leg sticking out.

"Oh, look," Thalia said. "They have a dog."

The man's eyes opened.

"They also have a librarian if you want one," he said. "Do you?"

"Not right now, thank you," Thalia said.

"Of course not," the man said, closing his eyes again.

"I have a question," I said.

The man's eyes opened.

"Are dogs allowed in this library?" I said.

"Absolutely not," the man said. "California law allows only companion dogs in public buildings. That dog is no one's companion."

"Then why is there a dog behind you?" I said.

"That's the question," the man said. "Why is there a dog behind me? Ms. Torres, have you an answer for that?"

"No," the golden woman said.

The man took a pencil and made two precise little hash marks on a paper in front of him.

"Does he like to be petted?" Thalia asked.

"I've never asked him," the man said, making another hash mark.

"I've got another question," I said. "Is there a tarantula in here?"

"Not to my knowledge," the man said, making yet another mark. "There is, however, a book on tarantulas in the children's section. J597.431, if you are interested."

"No, thanks," I said. "I already know as much about them as I want to."

Thalia went over and knelt beside the desk.

"Hi, boy. Hi, boy," she said, holding out her hand.

Something big and yellow and shaped like a dog's head raised off the floor, sniffed Thalia's fingers, and went back down with a *whuf*. The head was attached to a body the size of smallish pony, equipped with a set of immense feet and a tail that, unlike the rest of the animal that owned it, was fluffy. I had no idea what breeds it might have been descended from. Maybe it *was* part pony.

Thalia went on petting the head and whispering, "Hi, boy."

"I've got another question," I said. "Is this a real library?"

"Yes," the man said, and he made a mark.

"Why do you keep making marks every time we ask you things?" Thalia said, still scratching the big yellow head.

"Because this is reference week," the man said. "I must

keep statistics on all the questions I am asked." And he made another mark.

The dog-thing decided to get better acquainted with Thalia. He shambled to his feet and came out from behind the desk to lick her face.

"Is he your dog, sir?" Thalia asked.

"No," the man said. "I believe I said as much before. But I have no objection to answering the same question twice." He wrote down the next mark.

"Boozer isn't anybody's dog," the golden woman said. "He just lives here in town."

"I wish you'd waited for them to ask, Ms. Torres. Now I can't make a mark on this form," the man said.

"Hi, Boozer. Hi, boy," Thalia whispered again.

"Wait, I have a question," I said. "If it's illegal, why is he in here?"

"Thank you," the man said, making another mark. "Now, to answer your question, I don't know. The library seems to be on his circuit. He visits more or less regularly and stays for long periods. I should add, however, just in case you are here as spies from the city council or library administration, that he does so absolutely without my approval."

The door opened and Rob came in.

"Hey, Erik," Rob said. "Hi, Teri."

"Good afternoon," the librarian said. Ms. Torres nodded.

"So, you took my advice, huh?" Rob said.

Boozer stopped slobbering on my sister and went over to say hi to Rob. When his face was good and wet with saliva, Rob stood and went over to the shelves.

"Now, let's see, where did I leave off?"

"741.02," the librarian said, and of course made another mark.

"Right," Rob said, pulling books off the shelves. When he had ten, he went over to the checkout machine and ran them through. Then he took them to the desk where Ms. Torres was sitting and put them down.

"Thank you," she said.

Rob went back and checked out another ten books, and then took them over to Ms. Torres.

"What are you doing?" I asked when he'd done this three times and showed no intention of stopping.

"Increasing circulation," Rob said. "By the way, Erik, who wrote *King Lear*?"

"William Shakespeare," the librarian said, and made another mark.

"What's the capital of California?"

"Sacramento."

"How many grains of sand are on top of the picnic tables in the park right now?"

"Three thousand two hundred and forty-six."

"How can you know that?" Thalia said.

"Are you going to prove me wrong?" the librarian said, writing down two marks.

"What's going on here?" I said.

"As I told you, reference week," the librarian said, adding the mark for my question.

"Erik told me once that all the decisions about who gets what in the library system—new books, staff, all that stuff—are decided by statistics," Rob said, dropping ten more books on Ms. Torres's desk. "Guadalupe Slough is always dead last in everything they count. The library system would like to shut down the branch, which would leave Guadalupe Slough with exactly nothing in city services except the fire station. So I'm on a one-man crusade to make sure that doesn't happen. Every day they're open, I check out a hundred books. Every time the library does reference week, I come in and ask a bunch of questions. If you're going to stay here, you should get library cards and join my crusade. If everybody did that, we'd get a new library eventually."

"But if we got a new library with lots of people in here, would they still let Boozer in?" Thalia asked.

"Good question," Erik the librarian said, making a mark.

Boozer lay back down and sighed.

"Doesn't anybody besides you and Boozer use the library?" I asked Rob.

"Another good question," Erik said, marking it. "The answer, if I may interrupt and so include it in these statistics, is yes. To pay their utilities bills. Also, story time has a small but dedicated following. For the rest, not so much. Guadalupe Slough is a very small service area, and most people who live here do not seem to feel that the library we have meets their needs."

"Which is a shame, because Erik is really a hell of a reference librarian," Rob said. "The weirder it is, the more likely he is to know it."

"You are very kind," Erik said.

"Go on, ask him something," Rob said.

"I'm used to smart people," I said. "A librarian who knows what he's talking about is not something that would impress me. I mean, aren't you supposed to?"

"Yes," Erik said, and made a hash mark.

But Thalia wanted to play. "Okay," she said. "Umm . . . who was Glenn Miller?"

"American bandleader of the 1930s and '40s whose light plane, a UC-64 Norseman, disappeared while crossing the English Channel en route to a concert he was to play for the troops in Paris, December 14, 1944," Erik said. "You mean that Glenn Miller?"

"Yes," Thalia squealed. "But what was his biggest hit?"

"I can look that up on my phone," I said.

"It has been conclusively demonstrated that reference questions can be answered faster from printed sources than from electronic ones," Erik said. "And I, within my limits, am faster than print. Anyway, the answer to your question is probably 'Tuxedo Junction,' which sold more than 115,000 copies in its first week of release in 1939, but I'm not absolutely sure." And Erik made two more marks.

"Don't get him started," Ms. Torres said.

"Ms. Torres, this is a tax-supported institution," Rob said. "The more questions we ask him, the better return the people of this city get on their money."

"Sure, but if you get him going, he won't shut up till closing time, and I'll be the only one around to listen to it,"

Ms. Torres said. "You people can leave whenever you want. I can't."

"Life is a bitter, meaningless joke, Ms. Torres," Erik said. "It has cast you up like wretched refuse of this teeming slough and set you to work with me, a fate you did not deserve. I hope you know you have my sympathy."

"Karma," Rob said.

"If by karma you mean the preposterous notion that something Ms. Torres did in a previous life requires her to work with me to atone for it, nonsense," Erik said. "Karma, truly understood, is much like the Christian doctrine of original sin, properly understood. That is, merely humanity's inherent tendency to screw up. It is the force that causes communism to degenerate into state terrorism, and capitalism to degenerate in oligopoly. There is nothing to be done about it, and that is one of the reasons why life is a bitter, meaningless joke and certainly not Ms. Torres's fault."

"Now you've done it," Ms. Torres said. "Now he'll be going on for the rest of the afternoon."

I thought that might be kind of interesting, but I was tired and starting to feel annoyed that Daddy hadn't called yet, so I picked up a couple of library card applications and told Thalia to come on.

"Good-bye, Boozer," Thalia said as we left.

Boozer snuffled. He might have been saying good-bye.

"Please come back," Erik said. "This is the last day of reference week, but we will be conducting one again in six months. I hope you will not wait until then to return. And if you have a mother, father, or any adult willing to claim you as their own, Ms. Torres will be happy to issue you library cards."

He put his feet back up on the desk.

"See you tomorrow," Rob said, leaving with us.

"Lucky me," Ms. Torres said from behind a stack of slightly fewer than one hundred books.

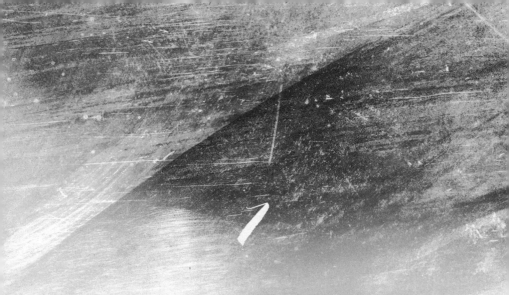

"That man is the strangest excuse for a librarian I have ever met in my life," I said.

"That's why he's here," Rob said. "The library system uses this place as a punishment, because nothing ever happens here."

"But what's he being punished for?" Thalia said.

"You may have noticed Erik is kind of a wise guy," Rob said.

"If anyone's being punished, it's that Ms. Torres," I said. "Locked in with that man all day."

"She has Boozer, though," Thalia said.

"That is hardly enough to compensate for a fate like that," I said.

"Well, it's time for me to go back home and commit literature," Rob said. "See you guys later. And say hi to your mom for me."

"We will," Thalia said.

"Well, what'll we do now?" I said when Rob was gone. I wanted to do something to pass the time until Daddy called—which had to be soon now—but the empty street didn't offer anything in the way of inspiration.

"Let's go to the beach." Thalia said.

"The beach," I said. "There is no beach here. There's only mud."

"Then let's go to the mud," Thalia said.

❧

Actually, there was a sort of beach just beyond the marina, where the mud turned to salt-crusted sand. It was a pale, gritty Martian landscape where patches of a low, reddish-green plant spread out like a nameless disease. A wide, flat ribbon of dust ran through it, labeled BIKE TRAIL by a couple signs. The trail ran north along the edge of the bay and out of sight in the direction of a big city. There were no bikes on the path—there was no one else to be seen—but within a mile to the east was the freeway, and it was full. It was like looking at another world through a sheet of dirty glass.

To the north, I could see a low bridge, and beyond it, wrapped in the mist, I saw two clumps of tall buildings facing each other across the water. One of them had to be San Francisco, but what the other, the one the bike path seemed to lead to, might be, I had no idea.

"Troy," I muttered.

"What?" Thalia said.

"That city up there on the right," I said. "You can't see the tops of the skyscrapers because of the fog. It makes me think of Troy. The topless towers of Illium."

"If that's Troy, then where are we?" Thalia said.

"To paraphrase Mama, we're in the Greek camp," I said. "With our boats pulled up on the beach. They've been there for ten years, so long they've sunk into the mud. We're stranded, just like they were."

"Stranded in the right place, though," Thalia said.

"No, we are not," I said.

"I kind of like it," Thalia said. "We have a town dog and our own spider. Try to cheer up, Elly. There's got to be more good stuff about this place."

That was not what I needed to hear. Something in the cheerful way she said it made me feel just how trapped I was.

"Thalia, you are so full of it," I said. "This place is a loony bin. We've got a crazy man with guns running around.

We've got a mean old man with a baseball bat threatening to attack us. We're living next to a bunch of drunks pretending to be poets and artists, and did I mention we're broke? We're sinking in quicksand and you want me to admire the view."

"It's gonna get better, Elly," Thalia said in a soft little voice.

"Get the hell away from me," I spat, because it was better than smacking her stupid cheerful face. I strode up the long, wide trail that led to the city in the mist.

"Elly," Thalia shouted after me, but she knew better than to follow.

I was so angry I didn't even care where I was going. And it might be that I was going nowhere. The topless towers never got any closer. And the weird flat landscape, with the quiet bay on one side and the freeway on the other, never changed.

Daddy, Daddy, Daddy, Daddy, Daddy, I kept thinking. *Daddy, Daddy, Daddy, Daddy, Daddy, get me out of here.*

After a while, I sat down to rest. I turned my back to the freeway and looked out across the water. A thick clump of dry reeds rattled in the soft wind, and a few seagulls glided low, looking for food, I guess.

Trapped. I was absolutely trapped. Daddy would never

call. I had no money of my own, and no way to get any. No way to get home. I might as well have been marooned on the dark side of the moon as in this strange, ugly place.

There was no one around, no one to hear me. I cut the empty quiet with my scream.

"Hey, excuse me, are you all right? Can I help?"

A boy about my age came out from behind the reeds. He was tall, golden-skinned, and his arms were ropes of lean muscle. He held a knife in his hand.

"Stay away from me, stay the hell away from me," I said, backing up.

"No, wait, it's cool, I was just trimming some driftwood," he said, putting the knife in a sheath on his belt. "Check it out if you don't believe me."

"I don't give a damn what you were doing," I said. "Stay away from me."

"Okay," he said.

I wanted to run, but how far could I get? And I didn't want to turn my back on him. So I stood up and started walking backward.

The boy stood at the side of the trail watching me. I started feeling safer—I was opening the distance, and keeping my eye on him and his knife—and then I tripped and fell over backward, with my leg under me. When I got up, cursing a blue streak, my ankle hurt.

More cursing.

I started hopping away.

"Hey," the boy called. "Can I give you a ride?"

I stopped hopping. My ankle was hurting more with every step. I was at least two miles from the spot where I'd left Thalia. I'd never get back on my own unless I crawled. Crawled away from a young man who'd come out of nowhere with a knife in his hand. And there was no one around but us.

The boy stopped waiting for my answer. He went back behind the reeds and then came out with an old, old child's wagon with a stump of weathered wood teetering on top of it.

"I can leave the wood and take you instead," he said.

I didn't answer him.

"Look," the boy said. He removed the stump and set it down near the reeds—God, he was strong. Then he took out his knife and hid it under the stump. "Now can I help you?" he said.

Something about that little rust-red wagon made him seem a lot less threatening.

I nodded, and he came closer, dragging the wagon

behind him like the world's biggest five-year-old.

I relaxed a little.

"I'm Carlos," he said. "Carlos Gonzales. *Servidor de usted.*" And he sort of shrugged.

"I don't speak Spanish," I said.

"Just means 'at your service,'" Carlos Gonzales said. "Where did you park your car?"

"I walked," I said.

"All the way from the slough?"

"I'd say that's obvious, wouldn't you?"

"Well, you don't live in town, so I figured you drove."

"I do live there, actually," I said. "For the moment."

"Then hop in and I'll take you back," he said.

"Elektra Kamenides," I said. "Thank you for your help."

I sat hunched in the wagon with my hurt leg sticking out in front. It was uncomfortable, but what else was I going to do?

Carlos pulled, the wagon squealed, and off we went.

"Where are you from?" Carlos asked.

"Mississippi."

"Wow," he said. "I never met anybody from Mississippi. That's pretty cool."

"What's cool about it?"

"It just is," Carlos said. "You must have just gotten here."

"Yes."

"I've lived in the slough all my life," Carlos said. "I've never been farther away than San Francisco."

"What's that big city across from it, the one on this side of the bay?" I said.

"That's Oakland."

"What were you doing out here?"

"Like I said, I was carving. I'm an artist. I have a commission."

"What kind of artist?"

"I work in wood that I find around. I do different things with it."

It was going to be a long trip in his wagon. I decided to find out more.

"You said your last name was Gonzales. Are you related to Mr. Gonzales? The one who hates white people?"

Carlos laughed. "My grandfather," he said. "*Mi abuelito*. But he's really a pussycat."

I had my own ideas about that but felt it was better not to express them as long as I was dependent on Carlos Gonzales for transportation. So I said, "Oakland. Where Gertrude Stein was from."

"Who?"

"Gertrude Stein. Experimental writer of the early twentieth century," I said. "Came from Oakland, lived in Paris. Collected a lot of famous artists before they were famous. Picasso, if you've heard of him."

Ooops. That sounded snider than I'd meant it to. But Carlos just laughed.

"Oh, *that* Gertrude Stein," he said. "And yeah, I've heard of Picasso. But I'm more into Diego Rivera. You know his murals?"

"I don't think so."

"He was more or less married to Frida Kahlo."

"Oh, *that* Diego Rivera," I said, because I did know Frida Kahlo's strange and beautiful work. How could I have forgotten Mexico's most famous male artist, whom she'd been in love with?

"Do you ever do murals?" I asked.

"Yep. I did that big one on El Diner. But I'm doing mostly sculpture now," Carlos said.

I recalled the four sculptures in the library that all had the same woman's face.

"How about those sculptures in the library?"

"Not mine," Carlos said. "My abuelito's. He keeps carving my grandmother. He really misses her."

"How'd they end up in the library?"

"Erik says they're a special collection. You can check one out and take it home with you for three weeks," Carlos said.

"Just check out a statue and take it home," I said.

"I guess you could check out all four if you wanted to," Carlos said. "No one ever does, though. They just sit there."

"But why are they in the library at all?"

"Because Erik thinks they're great," Carlos said. "He thinks my grandpa's a real artist. And says it's part of his job as a librarian to preserve my abuelito's work so it can be recognized."

"He also says no one ever checks anything out there," I said.

"Just Rob," Carlos said.

We didn't say anything much to each other for a long time after that. While Carlos dragged me along the bike trail, I watched the red-green plants slowly pass us by and listened to the quiet sound of the frothy little waves that tickled at the shore. Guadalupe Slough inched closer.

Finally, I remembered my manners.

"This is really very nice of you," I said. "I don't know how I would have gotten back without your help. I'm sorry if I was snarky."

"Around here, we look out for each other," Carlos said.

People in Mississippi looked out for each other, too.
But you had to have come from there. You had to belong
before you could belong. I had belonged, and I would
again. Somehow I'd get back and I'd pick up my life, and
this would just be a thing that had happened. But I had to
admit that what Carlos had said seemed to be true. This
place was strange, and the people were stranger, but they
were looking out for each other. And they were looking
out for me too, even though I didn't belong.

The sun was starting to slant down toward a shining
bank of fog hanging low in the west by the time my ride
pulled up in front of the barge. Carlos helped me lift myself
out of the wagon.

"Well," I said. "Thank you again. It was very kind of you
to help. I'm sorry you have to go back for your wood and
your knife."

"You're welcome," Carlos said. "Also, *por nada.* See
you around, maybe."

"Maybe," I said. "Like I said, I don't really know how
much longer I'll be here."

I limped up the ramp that led to our barge.

Behind me, I heard the rattles and squeaks of Carlos's
wagon heading back up the street toward the bike trail.

When I went into the trailer, the door to the bedroom was open and Thalia was lying on a bed. A bed we hadn't had that morning but did now. It was made of swoops of tarnished brass, and there was a fading scarlet spread on it, hanging down to the floor. It looked tacky, but it was definitely an improvement as a place to sleep, or to do what Thalia was doing, which was playing a game on her phone while she wiggled her feet between the bars of our new acquisition.

"Hi," Thalia said. "About time you got back."

"I was lucky to get back at all," I said. "I turned my ankle and had to accept a ride from a boy with a toy wagon."

"Was he nice?"

"Has Daddy called you?"

"No," Thalia said. "Mama called him, but he didn't answer. How's your ankle?"

"Where is she, anyway?" I said, ignoring Thalia's question.

"At Alix's, training," Thalia said.

"Training to do what?"

"Wash dishes," Thalia said. "She went over and asked for a job after breakfast and Alix told her she could start tonight. Then Alix sent Rob and Ralph over with this. She said she hasn't used it in thirty years and we might as well have it. Want to sit down? I can move."

"No," I said. "I'm calling Daddy. I want this room."

"You could say 'please,'" Thalia said.

"Get out. I'm hurt, and I'm mad, and I want five minutes alone with my father. Please."

Thalia got up and stamped past me.

I shut the door. I saw no sign of George, but that didn't comfort me. If I didn't know where he was, then he might be anywhere. Sooner or later, I was going to turn around and there he'd be with his hairy legs and his horrible slow walk and probably with a roach in his jaws. Or would I wake up and find him next to me on my pillow? I clenched my jaw and screamed behind my teeth.

"Daddy, please be home, please answer, and please, please get me out of here," I said as I punched in our old number.

If he didn't pick it up by the third ring, he wouldn't pick it up at all.

Ring.

"Daddy, Daddy, Daddy, please."

Ring.

"Daddy, Daddy, Daddy—"

Ring.

"Daddy—"

"Hello, Elektra."

My daddy's deep, powerful voice filled my ear, and I closed my eyes and smiled.

"About time," I said, laughing with relief. "Daddy, you would not believe where Mama has ended us up. I need to come home right away."

"I gather it's not quite what she expected?" Daddy said.

"Daddy, it's indescribable," I said.

"Describe it."

"Well, this place we're in is a sort of boat, but it's sunk in the mud, and there's a tarantula running around loose to eat the cockroaches, and there isn't even a shower curtain."

"That doesn't sound much like the California experience, does it?" Daddy said. "Seems a very odd place to be located in Silicon Valley."

"Daddy, the people we've already met include a retired brothel keeper, a suicidal failed poet, a lunatic with a gun collection, and a mean old Mexican man who hates white people. I've sprained my ankle. You have got to get me out of here before something really terrible happens."

Daddy was silent.

"Daddy?" I said. "What are you thinking about?"

"Elektra, let's talk," Daddy said.

Now I was silent.

"Your mother and I didn't rush into this," he said. "Your mother's behavior may make it seem so, but we didn't. We discussed it at length before she took off, and we agreed then that it would be best if you and Thalia stayed with her. At least for now."

"No, it isn't," I wailed.

"Your mother and I have come to the point where we agree on very little, but one of the few things we still see eye to eye on is our girls. We want what's best for you, even in this difficult situation. Not what's *good* for you; we know this isn't good. But *best*. And it's better for you to be where you are with her and Thalia than to try to endure life with me. I know that may seem hard to believe, but there are reasons why it's absolutely true."

"What reasons?" I said. "What reasons could you have for leaving me in a place like this?"

After a long minute, Daddy answered.

"There are factors in our decision that I can't tell you. You'll learn them in time, but I'm afraid all I can tell you right now is it really is for the best. Your best."

"Daddy, you're wrong. Please let me come home."

I heard his voice trembling.

"No, Elektra. Not now. It's not the time."

And then he hung up.

My fingers automatically punched in a saved number. I needed to talk to someone now—to hear the voice of a friend and pour my heart out.

Tracy's phone took me straight to "please leave a message." So did Iris's. So did Shawna's.

"Call me, call me *please*," I said each time. Then I stared at my useless little silver phone and I wailed. I keened like a whole Greek chorus. I didn't even notice at first when Thalia quietly opened the door and peeked in around it.

"Elektra," she said. "You want to cry together?"

I counted three tear streaks running down her cheeks. Her eyes promised more to come. She pushed the door open a little more and took a half step toward me.

I threw my phone at her. It hit her in the face and fell to the floor.

Thalia gasped and slammed the sliding door. I heard her sobbing in the front room.

"Leave me alone," I shouted by way of clarifying my feelings.

I bent over to pick up my phone.

George was coming out from under the bed, heading for dinner in the bathroom, I guess. I screamed and slid the door open so that he could escape. The only reason I didn't crush him was that the only thing more disgusting than George live would be George on my shoe. So I stood there, screaming, "I hate you," meaning everyone but mostly George while he ambled through the doorway. As soon as he was gone, I slammed it closed again.

I had to wait on a damned spider. That was what my life had come to.

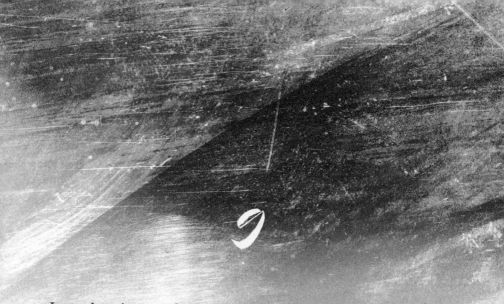

I raged against my fate, but my ankle hurt too much to do it upright for long. I had to get off my feet. I lay on the bed and the room got colder and darker.

This morning, I had hated the world, but I thought I understood it. Now I knew I didn't, and that made me feel naked and afraid. And it didn't matter a damn that in Greek literature people are always getting cut off from home and cast up on some unknown beach surrounded by strangers. They didn't like it, any of them, and neither did I.

I could not believe that my father didn't want me back. It made no sense. I was his, no matter what was going on between him and Mama. Then it hit me: he needed me. He didn't know it because he wasn't thinking straight. This whole thing had him so confused he didn't know what he really wanted. It was up to me to find my own way home.

Then he'd realize what he really felt, and I could help him.

It was time to start thinking about what to do next. I decided I'd better apologize to my little sister.

I turned on the light and limped down the hall, checking for George. No sign of him. The living room was dark. Thalia's deep breathing told me she was asleep.

I felt around for a light switch. When I found one, it didn't work.

"Crap," I said, which woke up Thalia.

"What are you doing?"

"Trying to find a light so I can apologize, damn it."

Thalia pulled on the light that worked.

"That was really mean," she said.

"It was," I said. "I'm sorry."

She moved over on the sofa and I sat down with her. We put our arms around each other.

"Daddy is a real bastard, isn't he?" Thalia said.

"No he's not. Don't talk that way."

"I will, 'cause he is," Thalia said. "It's the right word."

"What about Mama?" I said. "She's wanted to leave home for years. She's always been on Daddy to take a position at a better university."

"Yeah, but she never talked about leaving him," Thalia

said. "That was his idea before it was hers."

"Did she tell you that?"

"Some things you don't have to be told to know."

I decided not to tell Thalia what I'd realized about Daddy. She wouldn't believe it now. But the time would come when she'd see I'd been right. I took her hand. We'd held hands a lot back when we were small. Back then, it was always her idea. I'd be walking along the street or watching television, and I'd feel this small, warm bit of flesh fitting itself in between my palm and my fingers and I'd squeeze it. I did it now partly to say again that I was sorry and partly because it was a touch of home.

"What's going to happen to us?" Thalia said.

"I don't know," I said.

The cold was beginning to creep in through our paper-thin walls. I could hear the reeds rattle in the wind. Our light flickered, but decided to stay on, for now.

"Are you scared?" Thalia asked me.

"I wasn't. I am now."

"Me too."

Daddy once had a bumper sticker on his car that said WWOD—What Would Odysseus Do? The joke was that Odysseus was the guy nobody could outsmart; he was practical, underhanded, sneaky. The man of many turnings. Brave when he had to be—he was the one who hid inside the Trojan horse with a handful of his men and opened the gates to the Greek army in the middle of the night—but all he really wanted was to survive, to get home.

What would Odysseus do?

One thing I was sure of: he'd do whatever he had to.

I realized I was hungry.

"It's way past dinnertime," I said. "And I never had lunch. What about you?"

"I had some of the stuff from last night for lunch," Thalia said. "There's only a little bit left. I'm sorry."

"Don't be sorry," I said. "We're going to visit Rob."

"We are?"

"I'll bet there's all kinds of stuff left from his no-suicide party last night."

"We're just going to go over there and ask him to feed us?"

"If it hadn't been for us, he'd be dead now, right?" I said. "He owes us forever. He said so."

"It's too embarrassing."

"It's better than starving," I said. "Come on."

There was one light on in Rob's place. When we knocked, another came on over our heads.

"Hi," Rob said when he opened the door. "What's up?"

"We're hungry," I said.

"Come on in," he said. "If you don't mind breakfast for dinner, I can help you out."

Rob's kitchen was small and cluttered, but it had a tiny square table and four chairs. He moved books off the tabletop and onto the fourth chair. Then he got busy washing the dishes he was going to use to cook.

"Let me do that," I insisted.

"I'll dry," Thalia said.

"It's usually not quite this bad," Rob said. "I still haven't cleaned up everything from the party."

"You said you were going to commit literature," I said. "What did you get done? If you don't mind talking about it."

"Well, not so much, to tell you the truth," Rob said. "Hangovers and inspiration don't go together. But I did get a few lines down about you guys."

"About us?" Thalia chirped.

"I'm not going to inflict them on you," Rob said. "I don't even know why I mentioned them. Forget I said anything. How's George?"

"If we're going to be your muses, perhaps you ought to share what we've inspired in you," I said.

I was treading a thin line. I wanted him to think I was interested—that could mean future meals and who knew what else?—but I didn't want to distract him from dinner.

"Do you drink coffee?" Rob said. "I could use some."

He dragged a coffee maker out from somewhere and set it up while Thalia and I cleaned a frying pan, some plates, and some tableware. When we were done, Rob took over and started making eggs and toast. Nothing had ever tasted better to me, not even the chorizo that morning.

When we'd finished, he made us seconds, and I began to think about marrying him. Not really. But I was very grateful.

"So, do we get to hear the verses we inspired?"

"Just a few lines is all," Rob said.

"Please?" Thalia said.

Rob left and came back with a sheet of lined paper with words crossed out all over it.

"Just a few lines," he said again. He read in a soft voice,

"They came at end of day, alone and lost,

They stopped next door and got out of their car.

The tallest one, the mother, asked me where they were.

And I, up on my deck to watch the setting sun

And put a pistol to my head when day was done,

Was rescued by the lost ones . . ."

"That's all I got."

Sophocles it wasn't, but I smiled.

"Finish it," I said.

"Maybe tomorrow," Rob said.

"Let's do the dishes," Thalia suggested, and we did, while Rob dried and put things away. My ankle hurt, but my stomach didn't. One problem solved, Odysseus.

Looking at the dent we'd made in the kitchen mess, I had an idea.

"Rob, Thalia and I could clean this place up for you."

He thought that over.

"I couldn't pay you much," he said. "Plus there's a lot of stuff I wouldn't want you to touch. It looks like chaos, but I really know where everything is."

"We wouldn't touch anything you told us not to."

"Maybe the kitchen could use some work. How much cleaning could I get for twenty bucks?" Rob said.

"The whole thing," Thalia said.

I nodded.

"You're hired," he said.

"I need to ice my ankle. We'll come back tomorrow," I said. I wondered where I was going to get some ice.

Rob handed me and Thalia each a ten.

"On account," he said. "See you tomorrow."

The store was closed, but El Diner was open. Thalia and I went in.

"Can I buy some ice?" I asked the waitress. "I twisted my ankle."

"You want to buy ice?" she said. "Wait here."

And she came back in two minutes with a small bag filled with ice cubes.

"Take it," she said.

She was tall and beautiful and her face seemed familiar somehow.

"Thank you," I said. "Are you Carlos Gonzales's sister?"

"Cousin," she said. "You know him?"

"I met him today," I said. "He's very nice."

The cousin shrugged.

"He's okay," she said. "A little weird. He should be in San Francisco or Berkeley if he's going to do that artist stuff."

"What's your name?"

"Victoria," she said. "Tell him I said hi."

"Thanks again for the ice."

I limped out with Thalia beside me.

"At least people are nice here," Thalia said as I sat on the tiny living room couch with the bag of ice in a towel wrapped around my throbbing ankle.

"Yeah," I said. "A little off the wall for every day, but, yeah."

Thalia returned to her game, and I lay back and tried to relax. But now that I had had food, ten dollars in my pocket, and a job to go to tomorrow, I also had time to think about Daddy.

My mind kept running over his words, looking for something I'd missed, some way of understanding. He had stopped loving Mama? That was bad, very bad, but still, something between them, between grown-ups. I was his daughter, damn it. Didn't that count for something? It must, but what? Where did I fit into his life?

By the time Mama got home after midnight, my ankle felt a lot better. I've always been a fast healer.

Mama looked wiped out.

"How was it?"

"Hard," Mama said. "I thought I knew everything there was to know about washing dishes. I was wrong."

"Why are you home so late?" Thalia said. "I thought the restaurant closed at eleven."

"The kitchen closes then," Mama said. "But we still have to break down the steam tables and wash the oven racks. You have to wash everything. It takes another hour. But Alix was very pleased with the way things looked when I was finished. And we're going to eat like queens as long as I'm working there. Come on, kids, you must be starving."

She had a couple bags of stuff in her arms, and she set them down on the kitchen table.

I limped over to it. It was the first time Mama noticed my ankle. That's how tired she was.

"Elektra, what happened?"

"I'm fine," I said. "I just stepped on it wrong this afternoon."

"Let me take a look," Mama said.

"It's fine," I said. "I got some ice from the restaurant."

"We had dinner with Rob," Thalia said. "He made it. And tomorrow we're going to clean up his kitchen for him for ten dollars apiece."

"My God, how the money rolls in," Mama said. "So, are you guys still hungry?"

We were.

"Wow." Thalia had started going through the bags. "Even ice cream."

"No, no, no," Mama said. "Gelato. Imported authentic Italian gelato. Mere ice cream is not on the menu."

"Can we have some?" Thalia said.

"Why not?" Mama said. "Life is uncertain. Eat dessert when you can."

It was close to two when we finally went to bed. Thalia turned on her side, crossed her arms across her chest, and slid straight into sleep. Mama snored like a beached walrus for the first hour or so. Then she quieted and I was able to join them.

Just before I did, my mind showed me a picture of an ancient Greek ship, lying alone and dismasted on a beach somewhere. It had eyes painted at the bow, and black seagulls were slicing the sky overhead. Next to the eyes was the name of the ship.

Elektra.

WWOD?

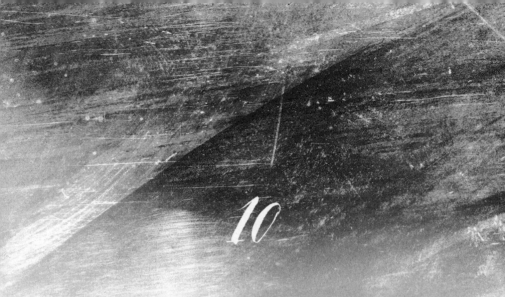

10

When I woke up, Daddy's abandonment still surrounded me like the black shades of Hades, but I pushed it back as far as I could. Odysseus never complained unless he thought it would do him some good. At least I knew what I had to do now, even if I didn't know how I was going to do it.

I realized I didn't know what day it was. I looked at Mama still fast asleep and at Thalia snuggled up against me. We were warm, but I was bugged by the fact that I'd lost track of time. I decided to find out, and I got up.

"Uh-uh," Thalia protested without really waking up.

I checked my phone. It told me it was just after nine in the morning on Sunday. I went down the hall to the— hurray—spiderless, roachless bathroom and took a quick shower. I found some fresh clothes and ate something delicately flavored and unidentifiable for breakfast.

Then I went next door to Rob's.

"I'm here to get started," I said when he opened the door.

"Cool," he said.

There's a kind of pleasure in cleaning up someone else's messy house. It's almost creative. Plus, I found out fast that whatever filing system Rob had for his papers and books and junk, he had no system at all for his kitchen. Whenever I asked where a thing went, he either shrugged or asked me where I thought would be good. I'd only planned to clear off the surfaces and mop the floor, but before long, I was tearing his cabinets apart and rearranging things to suit myself, which involved first washing most of what I found. By the time Thalia showed up, the place was even messier than it had been.

"Was there an explosion?" she asked when she came in.

"Just get busy," I said, and she did.

One thing about my kid sister is that she's a demon when she has a project in front of her. Rooting around under the sink, she found an unopened container of cleanser and attacked the sink with it. Then she cleaned the window, inside and out, and the wall behind the refrigerator. It turned into a game for us: who could find the next thing to clean? And we even started to laugh.

"Oh, my God, have you ever seen so many spider webs?"

"Gotcha beat. There's mouse turds down here."

There's a point in any cleaning project when the balance starts to tip toward actually making progress and, after three or four hours, we were there. Washed things disappeared into their new, cleaner homes. Odds and ends of packaged food either went to a designated pantry or into the trash, depending on their expiration dates. By four o'clock, we had that damn kitchen shining. At the end, we hung his collection of coffee cups from a package of unused hooks we'd found next to the oatmeal and shoved his four unmatched wooden kitchen chairs up against the red Formica table.

"Perfect," I said.

Thalia looked around. "It needs something."

She went outside and was back in a few minutes with her hands full of local weeds, which she proceeded to fashion into a bouquet using a slightly broken coffee mug as a vase. She set it in the center of the table.

"Too fussy," I said.

"It's beautiful," Thalia said.

"Beautiful, but not Rob."

"Let's let him decide." She went to fetch him from the rooftop deck where he'd gone to write.

He was carrying a clipboard with some lined paper on it and a battered paperback into which he'd been sticking Post-its.

"I have no words," Rob said when Thalia led him into our Temple of Clean. "It has never looked this good. I had no idea it could look this good. I can never use this room again."

"Hardest ten bucks I ever made," I said.

Then we gave him a tour of his shelves and cabinets. His eyes got bigger with each drawer we opened.

"What about the bouquet?" Thalia said at last. "Yes, or no?"

Rob sat down at the table.

"It's beautiful," he said. "But the sorrel is tickling my nose."

"Which one's the sorrel?" Thalia asked.

"The clover one with the little yellow flowers," Rob said.

Thalia plucked the sorrel out of her creation. This left a few tall stalks and some thick-skinned green and red stuff in the pot.

"Perfect," Rob said. "It's all perfect. But I fear I won't be able to keep it like this. I'll never remember where everything goes."

"Oh yes you will," I said. "I'm not seeing all this work wasted. Gimme those Post-its."

Rob turned them over to me, and I wrote down GLASSES, PANTRY, DISHES, PANS, and everything else that was neatly put away, and then I stuck them up.

"You will read and learn, sir," I said.

"Thank you," Rob said. "But I think you'd better come back next week. Just to see how my kitchen and I are getting along." Then he touched the bouquet. "I can get a poem out of this," he said.

That sounded like our cue to leave. We said good-bye and left Rob contemplating Thalia's work.

Outside, I high-fived Thalia.

"Ten bucks each, we're rich," I said.

"It's nice to see you cheerful," Thalia said. "Let's celebrate."

She led me down the street to the Mercado and over to the ice cream freezer. "Order up, I'm buying," she said.

When I'd picked out what I wanted, Thalia got two ice cream bars.

"Greedy," I said.

"One's for Mama," she said.

We got into the checkout line, and the clerk said, "How's the ankle?"

I looked up. It was Carlos. Boy, you put a guy behind a counter and you totally change how he looks.

"Much better," I said. "Thanks." Then I said, "Thalia, this is Carlos, the guy I was telling you about. The one with the wagon. Carlos, this is my sister, Thalia."

"How do you do," Thalia said. "You have a nice store."

"It is, actually," Carlos said. "We carry a lot of stuff you can't find most places. Mexican stuff, mostly, but all kinds of things."

"Is this your place?" Thalia asked.

"My family's," Carlos said. "I just help out around the edges. Mostly I work on my art."

"Did you get your piece of wood?" I asked.

"Oh, yeah," Carlos said. "I had a good talk with it all the way back to my studio. I told it it's going to be a tree again. Sort of a Brancusi one."

"I'm afraid I don't know much about the different species of trees."

Carlos smiled.

"Brancusi's an artist," he said. "Very smooth lines. Kind of streamlined. He did birds. Of course, birds are kind of streamlined anyway."

"Oh," I said. "Brancusi. Right."

"Come around to my studio in a week or so when I've had a chance to work on it," Carlos said. "I'd like to know what you think."

"We'd love to see your studio," Thalia said. "Where is it?"

"Just up on the roof of this place."

"That is so cool," Thalia said. "We'll come by."

"We'd better go before our ice cream melts," I said.

"Okay," Carlos said. "We'll set it up. Have a nice day."

On the way back to the marina, Thalia looked at me. "I think he likes you."

"Not interested," I said.

"Why not?"

Because I'm not going to be here that long, I thought. But I said, "He's too old, for one thing."

"Too old for one thing, too smart for another thing, and too nice for a third thing," Thalia said. "You're right, Elektra. You're not good enough for him."

"Eat your ice cream," I said. "And keep your thirteen-year-old opinions to your thirteen-year-old self."

"Brancusi," Thalia said, taking a bite of her bar.

We caught Mama just as she was getting ready to leave for her shift at Alix's.

"Oh, you dears," she said as she took the ice cream. "You absolute dears."

Thalia had the good grace not to take all the credit for

being thoughtful, and I had the bad grace not to give it to her. Let Mama think both her daughters were being nice to her; what could it hurt?

Then I had my own nice-daughter idea.

"Let us walk with you to work," I said.

The three of us sauntered through the quiet streets toward the restaurant. My ankle twinged just a little. Gulls called, and the calm gray bay glistened on our right as we strolled. The big ALIX's sign hung over the town a few blocks ahead.

"I've been taking inventory of myself," Mama said. "Trying to think of things I can do to make more money."

"I thought you came out here to be a writer," Thalia said.

"I did. I have. I will," Mama said. "But I have to get an income stream going until things start to break right for me. And there's no way to tell how long that will take. So far, I've come up with substitute teaching, working in a day care, and not much else."

"It's summer," I said. "No school. Plus, you don't have a car."

"I know. I'll have to get that taken care of," Mama said. "But I've got about five weeks before school starts. That's plenty of time."

Mama was starting to sound like Thalia, except her cheerfulness was forced and phony, which made me furious.

"Well, since we've been here, people have given us food, a tarantula, and a bed," I said. "Pretty soon someone will give you a car. Then all you'll need is gas and insurance and you can start your brilliant career substitute teaching. Ah, to dwell in possibility."

"We've got a job, Mama," Thalia piped up. "Mr. Schreiber wants us to clean his kitchen every week."

Mama ignored her.

"Elektra, I'm doing the best I can," she said.

"I know," I said. "That's what worries me."

Whap.

Mama's hand came soaring in from the left to connect with my face. It didn't really hurt, but the shock was electric. Neither of my parents had ever hit either of us before.

Mama looked like she couldn't believe what she'd just done.

"Thank you," I said, turning back the way we'd come.

"Elektra, I'm sorry," Mama said.

I didn't answer. I didn't want anything to do with Mama just then, or ever. But I meant it when I had thanked her. Mama had slapped my Odysseus into high gear. Five weeks? I'd be gone long before then. I didn't know how I was going to do it, but it was the only way ahead.

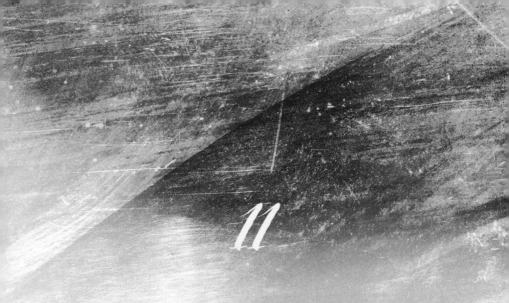

11

It took Odysseus ten years to get home from Troy. Ten years. But a lot of that time, he wasn't really trying. Just sitting around on an island with some goddess who'd taken a liking to him. I would do better.

This was my goal: to get back to Mississippi, back to Cleburne, and to walk in on my father and save him. Beyond that, I didn't have much of a plan, but that was all right. Once I was back home, things would start to happen for me.

To get back, I needed money, hundreds of dollars at least. That meant I needed to make some. Robbing a bank crossed my mind, but I rejected that right away since it would have required a getaway car. Also, I didn't know the location of any banks.

Around Guadalupe Slough, I'd seen kids about my age who seemed to have work. I would see what I could do.

But where was I to start looking? WWOD? I decided he would go to the library. Erik the librarian would be grateful for a real reference question.

When I got there, the door was half open, propped that way by Boozer. Anybody who wanted in or out had to step over him.

"*Murf*," he said as I did just that.

"Murf yourself," I said.

One thump of his tail, and he was back in that dreamland where dogs seem to spend most of their lives.

Inside, Erik and Carlos were leaning against the desk holding gigantic paper coffee cups and talking away. Erik was waving his hands around so much his coffee was sloshing, and Carlos was nodding at everything he said.

"The tree will have several levels of meaning," Erik was saying. "I know you grasp this, but I want you to make it explicit. The tree of knowledge, yes, but also the Meso-American tree of life. The world tree. All right here, in one great synthesis. Political, yes, but not superficial like so much art in public buildings."

"It's got to be comprehensible, though," Carlos said. "I want people to be able to look at it and understand it on some level as soon as they see it. Because it is public art."

"Okay, okay, but depth. I want it to have depth," Erik said. "Resonance."

"Excuse me," I said. "Do you have time for a reference question?"

"I always have time for reference questions," Erik said. "I live for them, actually. During working hours, which is what these present hours are. So please, Ms. Kamenides, ask away. I am anxious to be of any assistance whatever."

"How many of those have you had?" Ms. Torres called from the check-in desk across the room. "He's on a caffeine jag," she explained to me.

"Ms. Torres, you are perfectly well aware that I am capable of being like this with or without coffee," Erik said. "The chance to be of service to another in my role as librarian—*public* librarian, if I may say so—is, and should be, stimulation enough for any right-minded library employee. I invite you to experience it. Now, then, Ms. Kamenides, what is your question?"

"I was wondering if you knew of any work I could do around town," I said. "I need a job."

"Employment," Erik said. "How old are you?"

"Sixteen," I said.

"That presents difficulties," Erik said. "There are very few sources of employment for someone of that age. Had you been here in May, you could have applied to work here through a city program that provides summer employment to teens. But you were not, and we had no applicants, so the position has gone unfilled."

"What about where you work?" I said to Carlos. "I met your cousin, and she doesn't look any older than I am."

"But her parents own the market," Carlos said. "That's a whole different set of rules." Then he added, "Of course, you could marry me and get into the family that way."

"No, thanks," I said. "See, back in Mississippi, we all get married real young. I've already buried three husbands and divorced the rest. I'm pretty much done with men."

Carlos laughed. "Oh, well."

"How mobile are you?" Erik asked, which I understood to mean *Do you have a car?*

"Not very," I said. "It has to be someplace I can walk to. Or take a bus, I guess."

"Dear, dear, dear, dear, dear," Erik said. "Very difficult."

"Listen, Erik," Carlos interrupted, "I'm going to go and get that piece of wood I found a couple days ago when I met her. I'll bring it by, okay?"

124

"Excellent," Erik said. "I look forward to it."

"Sorry about your husbands," Carlos said as he stepped over Boozer and out into the pale yellow light.

"Thanks," I said.

WWOD?

"Is there any way I can apply for that teen employment program now?" I said.

"You can," Erik said. "For next summer."

I looked around the tiny, dark library.

A poster on the wall by the checkout desk showed four teenagers smiling like loons, surrounded by carts of books. It said, JOIN TEENSERVE. ASK HERE.

So I did.

"What's TeenServe?" I said. "Does it pay anything?"

"TeenServe is the library's volunteer opportunity program for teenagers, and no it does not pay," Erik said. "It merely provides you with the opportunity to earn the service hours you will require for our high school graduation while performing various simple library tasks in the company of other young people. And no, this branch does not have a functioning chapter. No one is interested."

"I am," I said. "Anyway, I might be. Is this another one of your statistics?"

"Yes," Erik said. "Indeed the administration is quite interested in the success of TeenServe. Or perhaps, I should say that they are interested in the absolute absence of success that TeenServe has had at this branch. I suspect that if there were someplace worse to send me than here, they would do it."

"They should send him to the main branch and make him work on the reference desk," Ms. Torres said. "It's all he likes doing."

"Ms. Torres, your words are as unjust as they are wounding," Erik said. "It is a flaming brand of eternal shame to me that no one wants to join TeenServe."

"Well, I'll be your TeenServe if you pay me," I said. "I'll get a library card and I'll come in here and check out a hundred books a day like Rob. I'll even get my sister to join. Just don't tell her about our deal."

"Hmm," Erik said. "What would you charge me?"

"Ten dollars a meeting," I said.

"Done," Erik said, and he chuckled. "Shall we say the first meeting was today?"

I held out my hand. Erik put a ten-dollar bill into it.

"A pleasure doing business with you, Ms. Kamenides," he said. "I look forward to our next monthly meeting in August."

"Me too," I said.

"You're corrupting her," Ms. Torres called.

"No, Ms. Torres. In fact, she is corrupting me," Erik said.

"Good point," Ms. Torres said.

I gave a last pat to Boozer, who hadn't moved since I got there, and said good-bye.

"Good-bye, Ms. Kamenides. Thank you for your public-spirited attitude. We look forward to seeing you again soon," Erik said, taking another huge gulp of coffee.

"Hmpf," Ms. Torres said.

"*Mrph*," Boozer agreed.

So now I had twenty bucks toward getting home.

I needed to stash it. I'm not a huge spender, but sometimes money spends itself. I'd go back to the place I presently called home and, if Thalia wasn't there, I'd find a hole in the wall or something, somewhere to hide it.

When I got back to the marina, I saw our old Volkswagen with both doors wide open and its little curved hood up. That did not look good. I ran to the car.

"Hey," I said. "Hey, that's our car."

Ralph stood as I approached, held a lump of metal over his head, and waved it.

"What are you doing to our car?" I squawked.

"Solenoid. I found it," he said.

There were some screwdrivers lying around and a couple wrenches.

"That's the thing about Ralph," Rob said, emerging from the other side of the car. "Once he starts looking for something, he doesn't quit."

"But you broke into our car," I said.

"Wasn't locked," Ralph said.

Mama must have forgotten. And anyway, what did it matter? At this point, the whole car was an anti-theft device.

"Do you have the key?" Rob said. "We need to see if it'll start."

I happened to know that Mama had left the keys hanging by our front door.

I watched while the two guys changed out the part and put everything back together. Then I went and got the key.

Ralph turned it, and the ugly little car's engine barked, snapped, and started.

"Solenoid," Rob said.

Ralph turned off the engine and handed me the key.

I was elated. Having the car back felt like a huge step forward. Then I thought of the twenty dollars in my pocket.

"How much do we owe you?"

"How much you got?" Ralph said.

"About ten dollars," I said.

"Not enough. Better not pay me," he said with a grin. His teeth were yellow and there were gaps in them.

He gathered up his tools.

"My mother's going to want to repay you somehow," I said.

"You taught me how to dance that dance," he said. "See you."

He dumped his tools into an old backpack and walked off in the direction of the ruin of bricks where the swallows lived.

"Boy," Rob said. "That's more than he usually says all day."

"I have to admit, that was kind of amazing," I said.

"Sometimes I suspect he isn't insane at all. Just sane in a totally unique way," Rob said. "No. No, forget I said that. That's patronizing." He looked angry with himself. "He went to war and came back broken. Always on first watch. But something inside him keeps trying to get better."

"How does he live?" I asked.

"You mean how does he get money?" Rob said. "He's got some kind of government disability, but I don't think he spends it. I'm pretty sure he doesn't grasp that he has it. As far as I know, he lives on what he makes from scrounging. He's good at that."

Well, that was a thought. Maybe I could do that, too, between cleaning Rob's kitchen and checking out library books. Aluminum cans might get me home by the end of summer if I worked hard enough. Maybe Ralph could give me some pointers. And something else crossed my mind. If he had money that he wasn't using, maybe he wouldn't mind it if someone else did.

"He's really very nice, isn't he?" I said. "I want to get to know him better."

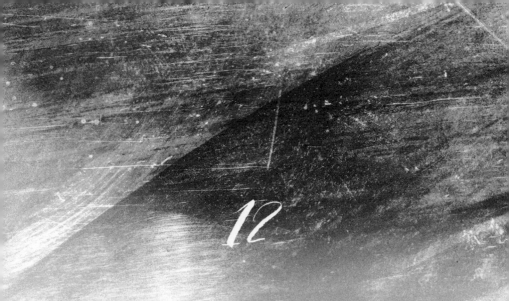

12

I found a place to stash my cash in the kitchen. I taped each bill to the underside of the silverware drawer. When was the last time you looked at the underside of a kitchen drawer? Odysseus would have been proud.

Once I had done that, it occurred to me to wonder where Thalia was. If she wasn't here or at the library or out front with Ralph and Rob, where was she?

George came by, slowly and steadily proceeding across the living room floor on his obscene hairy legs.

"Hey, you, where's my sister?" I said, but he ignored me.

I went out and climbed up on the balcony or whatever it was to see if she might be there. I hadn't been to our little terrace before, and nothing I saw inclined me to return. It was thick, warped plywood with some scraps of unmatched linoleum covering most of it and weathered gray wood where the linoleum stopped. The one thing it did have was a view. You could see all over town from up there.

I looked all around but saw no sign of her. I decided not to worry. She'd probably found another stray dog to pet.

I looked out over the reeds toward the bay maybe a hundred feet away and watched ripples of tiny, froth-crested waves across the shallow gray water. It looked almost like the Aegean Sea, where we'd gone two years ago when Daddy was on sabbatical. The Aegean is so small and enclosed that it has hardly any waves at all. Apparently San Francisco Bay wasn't much different.

I thought back on that trip, and about Mama and Daddy together. How much Daddy had talked, how much Mama had tried to. We'd spent a lot of time with other scholars, writers, and people like that, nearly all of them Greek, and nearly all of them men. They'd almost fawned on Daddy, but Mama hadn't been much more than a piece of furniture, a piece of furniture who kept trying to talk. But she didn't speak Greek, and Daddy and his court hardly spoke anything else when they were together.

At the time, I hadn't thought much about it. Now I wondered how much that summer had to do with this one. Had that been when things had changed between Mama and Daddy? I couldn't really tell. But for the first time, I realized that Daddy had maybe not been so cool, excluding her that way. It wasn't like the people we met couldn't speak English. And Mama had been almost desperate to talk to some of the writers.

Maybe she had been lonely then the way I was lonely now. Maybe—I didn't like this idea—maybe Mama trying to get away to California wasn't much different from my trying to get away from it. Maybe.

But I was never going to understand until I got home and found out what was really going on with Daddy. I was not only furious about what had been done to me, but I was also curious as hell about what was really going on.

Then, in the distance, I saw Carlos and his little red wagon coming down the bike trail. There was something tall and teetery in it that looked like part of an old machine. Thalia was walking along beside him, helping balance it. The thing wobbled while the wind blew dust around them, and after a while, Boozer wandered up from wherever he'd been and joined them, too.

I watched until they disappeared into the little nest of buildings that was Guadalupe Slough.

Well, Thalia had always made friends fast.

A little while later, I saw her coming back down the street alone. She waved. So did I.

"Hey, Elektra, Carlos is neat," she hollered when she was within hollering distance.

I am disinclined to conduct conversations at the top of my voice, so I didn't answer. That didn't stop Thalia. She went on talking, diminishing her voice slightly as she got closer, until by the time she was back on our yacht it was almost normal. Almost.

"I went for a walk to see where you'd gone yesterday and I saw him and we got to talking," she hollered up at me. "He'd found this old rusty engine part and I helped him get it onto his wagon, and then I balanced it for him and we talked all the way back. He said since we were hanging out anyway, he might as well show me his studio now if I wanted to see it and I did, so took me took me up there and he showed me some of his tools and things. And I'm sure now he likes you."

"Louder," I said. "I'm not sure everyone heard you."

"What everyone?" Thalia said. "Anyway, he kept asking me things about you."

"Thalia, shut up," I said.

"Well, maybe if you had a boyfriend you wouldn't be so

unhappy," Thalia said, climbing up the stairs to sit beside me on the balcony.

We hung our legs over the edge of the plywood and looked over the town.

"What good is a boyfriend going to do me?" Oops. I almost blurted out something about not staying that long. I covered myself with, "I didn't have one back home."

"Back home all the boys you liked liked someone else," Thalia said. "Out here you don't like anybody, and Carlos likes you. Anyway, I'm pretty sure he does. Isn't that an improvement?"

"No," I said. "Thalia, we're in a place where crazy people run around with guns that may or may not shoot. They give spiders as presents and they commit suicide at sundown because they're bad poets. Ex-hookers and old men with baseball bats. That's who lives here. Why would I want a boyfriend from a place like this?"

"Well, I like him," Thalia said.

"Well, I'm sorry, but I have better taste than that."

"You don't have taste, you're just a snob."

I decided not to answer that. When I had my bus ticket, I would leave a note and that would be my answer.

But Thalia kept talking.

"Even if you are a snob, you should like Carlos because he's an artist," she said. "That's better than a regular guy."

"Hah," I said. "Real artists treat women like dirt. Gauguin did, Picasso did. Andy Warhol did, and he didn't even like women. You aren't going to catch me hanging around a guy like that."

"But—"

"I declare this conversation stupid and over."

And in fact it was over, because T'Pring came up the street waving. She was wearing jeans and a T-shirt. I hardly recognized her at first with her belly covered.

Thalia and I climbed down to greet her.

"Hi," she said. "Antonio and I were wondering if you'd like to come over for dinner."

"Sure," Thalia said.

I couldn't think of any reason to turn down free food.

"Come on, then," she said, cocking her head.

So we went with her. We walked up the street along the line of beached boats and barges until we came to one that had once been a big cabin cruiser. It lay slightly on its side, and running from its bow to its stern were long lines of cord covered with little triangular flags that were red, yellow, green, and blue.

"Tibetan prayer flags?" I asked.

"That's where the idea came from," T'Pring said. "But they're something my husband came up with. Mexican party flags. See how there's a shape cut out of each one?"

I did. Some had bottles. Others were smiling faces. Some were knives and forks. All kinds of things.

"There's a Mexican folk art called *papel picado*," T'Pring said. "Little squares of tissue paper with shapes cut out of them. Antonio thought it would be good to make something similar out of cloth. We hoist them whenever we're having a party."

"Is that what you're praying for, a good party?" Thalia asked.

"I suppose," T'Pring said. "Anyway, it's nice to pray for something you're so likely to get."

Antonio was standing on the deck with a beer bottle in his hand. He smiled at us.

"Permission to come aboard," T'Pring shouted.

"Permission granted," Antonio said, and he bowed.

We went down a steep little ladder into the cabin and saw that it had been decorated, too, hung with paper streamers and small lanterns that glowed vague, warm circles of light. There was a long, narrow table made of one beautiful piece of wood and even-more-narrow benches on either side of it. The smell of something delicious filled the cabin.

"Hey," Rob said. "Good to see you."

"Hi," Thalia said. "How's the poetry going?"

"Dylan Thomas used to say he worked all day to get two lines of real poetry," Rob said. "All I can claim is: I worked all day."

"I bet even Homer had bad days," Thalia said.

Antonio came into the cabin from the galley. He was carrying a big, bright clay pot full of whatever was making the wonderful smell.

"Ah," T'Pring said. "Mexican food à la Antonio."

"What is it?" Thalia said.

"Mexican food," Antonio said. "I'm Mexican, it's food."

"Sometimes Antonio just goes into the kitchen—excuse me, the galley—and makes something out of whatever he finds there," T'Pring said. "The only thing these culinary experiments have in common is that they're delicious. What can I give you to drink?"

Rob reached behind him and took a couple cans out of a small cooler. He held up something that was a cola and something else that wasn't.

"Red or white?" he said.

I said red and got the cola. Thalia said white and got the other.

Rob reached into the cooler again and pulled out three beers.

As we ate, a shadow appeared in the hatchway and another set of feet came down the ladder. They were attached to Carlos.

"Hey, cousin," Antonio said.

"Hey, all the good people are here," Carlos said, and he sat down next to me.

He was sitting very close to me. I shifted two inches toward Thalia. She pushed back. I stepped on her foot with my good one.

"Ouch, Elektra," she said.

Carlos slid an inch in the opposite direction.

"Crowded," he said.

Antonio's cooking was as good as it smelled. Beans, rice, some kind of sausage, and an amazing web of seasonings that made me realize I was hungrier than I'd thought.

"This is great," Thalia said. "I wish Mama could be here."

"So how's school, cuz?" Antonio asked Carlos.

"Got an art class for summer session," Carlos said. "Introduction to Sculpture."

"Sweet," T'Pring said. "Is it filling?"

"Won't know till the last day," Carlos said.

"Where are you taking it?" Thalia asked.

"He's not taking it, he's teaching it," Antonio said. "He's the one in this family with brains."

"You're teaching?" I said, because Carlos looked like he was still in his teens. "How old are you?"

"Nineteen," Carlos said.

"And you're teaching where?" I said.

"Guadalupe Community College," Carlos said. "This is my second time there. If my class fills."

"How can a nineteen-year-old teach at a community college?" I said. "Don't you need at least a master's degree for that?"

"Not absolutely," Carlos said. "Some fields you can get into with a BA."

"Which you've got?" Thalia asked.

Carlos shrugged.

"He finished high school at fifteen," T'Pring said. "The family sent him to Stanford to keep him off the streets."

I knew three things about Stanford University: it was very good, it was very hard to get into, and it was very expensive.

"Boy," Thalia said. "You must be real smart. We thought this place was just about retired hookers and old men with baseball bats, didn't we, Elly?"

"Whatever gave you that idea?" I said. Because while I didn't care what Carlos the geek with the little red wagon thought about me, Carlos the nineteen-year-old Stanford grad was different. Thalia was right. I was a snob.

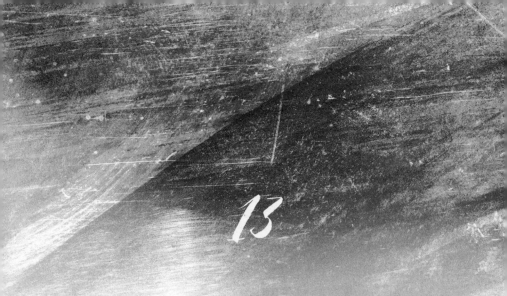

13

After dinner, Thalia volunteered to wash the dishes. That would have meant I had to help, but the galley was too small for more than one person. Besides, Thalia liked to wash dishes, especially other people's. When we had parties back in Mississippi, she always tried to help out the hostess.

She sang while she worked.

"Starlight,
Why you droppin' down on me?
Ain't there some place you would rather be?
Some place where lovers meet,
Some quiet lane or busy street?
Starlight,
Ain't it time for you to go away?
Find some place to settle down and stay,
Cottage small or Spanish castle tall,

'Cause I don't need your light at all.

My love has left me . . ."

Antonio pulled down a guitar from a hook on the ceiling and strummed along with her. T'Pring leaned across the table and smiled at her husband. It was a wonderful smile, the kind I used to see on Mama's face when she looked at Daddy while he was lecturing or making a really good point in conversation. I hadn't seen a smile like that for years.

Rob was sitting in his corner with his eyes closed, his glass half full, and his feet propped up on the table, turning his head back and forth in time to the music.

Beside me, Carlos was sketching us, one picture after another. T'Pring's smile, Rob's bliss, Thalia's faraway look. The guy had talent, I had to say that for him.

So he was smart, nice, handsome, tall, and gifted. I was leaving as soon as I had the money, but I couldn't help feeling like I would be missing out on something when I left.

Carlos shifted himself to get better light, and I caught a glimpse of what he was drawing. It was me, and I was dressed in a flowing gown. My arms were above my head and I was holding the moon in my hands. He'd drawn little stars beside it. Below my hips, my body disappeared into a sort of bouquet of stylized ocean waves that resembled the ones on Greek pottery.

Carlos saw me looking.

"Venus rising from the sea," he said.

"Aphrodite," I said, standing. "Venus was some damn Roman goddess."

There wasn't room in the cabin for me, so I went out on the stern, kicked off my shoes, and began to dance slowly and carefully. But not belly dancing. I began to twirl, one hand up to heaven, one hand down to earth.

I was praying for Mississippi. To be back there right now, this minute, dancing just as I was, on our deck under that moon with the deer watching.

I went on spinning while Thalia changed songs and Antonio's guitar stitched a web of notes around the words. It wasn't really music to whirl to, but somehow on the deck of that mud-locked boat and under that cool gray sky it kind of worked. And after a long time, the sky shifted for just a moment and the moonlight fell on me through a thin skein of cloud, and I could see Carlos standing in the hatchway smiling at me.

I stopped.

"So, you gonna just watch, or you gonna try it?" I said.

"I can't dance like that to this music," Carlos said. "But I can try something else."

He came toward me and put his arms up, inviting me to waltz.

We managed a slow dance to Antonio's guitar without falling over. And I liked the way his arms felt.

When it was done, Carlos stepped back and bowed.

"Thank you, milady," he said.

"That was pretty good," I said. "Surprised you knew how to do it."

Carlos laughed.

"Back in eighth grade, I was having trouble with math. Mom said if I didn't get at least a C, I had to take ballroom dancing. She thought it might help me pay attention in class. It didn't work."

"I'd rather dance than do pre-algebra almost anytime," I said.

"So would I," Carlos said, holding up his arms again.

I didn't count the number of dances we had. I was enjoying the vacation from worry too much to keep statistics on it. And it wasn't until we stopped that I realized my ankle was fine.

But I wasn't falling in love, or even in like. Okay, I was a little in like, but since I was leaving, it didn't matter. And if I had a sense that he was starting to feel something for me, then, fine. If he tried to kiss me, he wouldn't get to. But the dancing could go on all night as far as I was concerned.

But it didn't. After a while, the music stopped, and I thanked Carlos and we went back inside.

Rob was scribbling on an ancient roll of computer paper that must have gone back to the eighties. It was as yellow as old parchment and had little oblong holes along both sides of it. It reminded me of the papyrus scrolls the Greeks used to write on, back when Aristotle was hot stuff.

"Doughnuts," Antonio said.

"Fairies," Thalia said.

"Despair," T'Pring said.

Rob closed his eyes and repeated, "Doughnuts, fairies, despair. Okay . . ."

Then after a minute, he started scribbling. Antonio, Thalia, and T'Pring watched while he wrote, crossed out, and wrote again.

T'Pring looked at her phone.

"Time," she said.

Rob put down his pencil and read,

"There are no doughnuts.

The fairies have eaten them.

I snack on despair."

"Yay," Thalia said.

"Lame," T'Pring said.

"Another one," Antonio said.

"Another what?" I asked.

"Rob's speed-dating with the Muse," Thalia said. "We give him three words. He's got to come up with a haiku that uses each word in a separate line in two minutes."

"I just thought of this," Rob said. "I'm trying to train my mind to be open to what I think Theodore Roethke called 'the moment of wonder.'"

Carlos and I slid back into our seats at the table.

"Coastline," Antonio said.

"Camel walk," T'Pring said.

"Library," Thalia said.

"Got it," Rob said. He wrote like a demon for a minute then announced,

"I see no camel walk

This coastline, empty except

For the library."

"Awful," T'Pring said, putting her head on the table.

"Cool," Antonio said.

"Cool and fast," Thalia said.

They did four or five more. Rob looked more pleased with himself every minute.

"I'm onto something, I'm onto something," he said over and over.

"You guys try," Thalia said to me and Carlos. "I'll do the third."

"Okay, 'pencil,'" Carlos said.

I smiled innocently.

"Stade," I said.

"What?" Rob asked.

"Stade," I repeated. "Perfectly ordinary word."

"No fair," Thalia said. "That's not English, it's Greek."

"I accept the challenge," Rob said. "Give me my third word."

"Oh, 'Boozer.' Like the dog," Thalia said.

"Hah," Rob said. "Okay, start the meter running."

The five of us watched him scrunch his face up like a wet towel. His pencil was frozen in his hand. T'Pring's phone counted the seconds: 90, 91, 92, 93 . . .

Suddenly, Rob's pencil began to move.

"Time," T'Pring called, just as Rob jumped up and shouted,

"What is a stade?

I know no more than Boozer.

My pencil is still."

"Great save," Carlos said.

"But I called time," T'Pring argued.

"I say he made it," Antonio said. "It's like when you cross an intersection on a yellow light. If it turns red while you're in it, you're still legal."

"He made it, he made it," Thalia said.

"What is a stade, anyway?" Rob said.

"It's an ancient Greek unit of measurement," I said. "Six hundred feet."

"I still say no fair," Thalia said.

"I disagree completely," Rob said. "The whole point of doing this is to open me up to wonder. And I sure as hell was wondering what a stade was."

"And I'm wondering what you girls are doing here," Mama said from the hatchway. "It's midnight."

14

"It is?" I said.

"It is," T'Pring said.

"Yes, it is," Mama said. "And I repeat, what are you doing here so late?"

"We're celebrating your car getting fixed, Mama," Thalia piped up.

"What do you mean, the car is fixed?"

"Mr. Cummins found a solenoid and put it in and now it runs," Thalia explained.

Mama's face went through several changes like she was deciding which Greek theatrical mask to put on: tragedy, comedy, tragedy, comedy.

Thalia saw it, too.

"And Rob helped," she said.

Tragedy. Definitively tragedy.

"It's time to go home," Mama said.

Everyone had to stand so that Thalia and I could get out.

"Can we offer you a—" T'Pring said.

"Thank you," Mama said. "Good night, everyone."

Mama was bristling as we walked back to Slip 19.

"Mama, what's wrong?" Thalia said. "The car is really fixed. Now you can get a better job and drive to it."

Mama didn't answer at first. We heard nothing but the scuff of our shoes on the quiet street.

I couldn't believe I had lost track of time like that. It was like I'd been hanging out with the lotus-eaters who'd almost wrecked Odysseus's chances of getting home. But they'd had a narcotic, which they shared with some of Odysseus's crew. Maybe those guys on that boat were a bunch of lotus-eaters, too. Maybe—

We reached our place. It looked dank and dark. Like a temple someone had built to the goddess of lost hopes. We went in.

Mama turned on the light. I looked around for George. Thalia started defending Rob and Ralph again. Mama interrupted her.

"If the car works, that's wonderful," Mama said. "But it also incurs a burden of debt that I don't have a way to pay back right now. And frankly, I feel violated. Those men got into my car and did whatever they wanted to it. They did it without asking me, or even telling me that they were going to do it. That is not okay. That is absolutely wrong, whatever their motives were."

"But, Mama, they just wanted to help," Thalia said.

"And there's something else," Mama said. "I came home to a dark house. I had no idea where you were, or what might have happened to you. Do you understand why I'm upset? No, not upset. I'm angry. I want you girls to start treating me with a little more respect. Damn it, I deserve that much at least."

"I'm sorry, Mama," Thalia said.

I didn't say anything. As far as I was concerned, Mama had it coming.

"There's food from Alix's if you want it," Mama said, and she disappeared into the bathroom.

The steady hiss of the shower started.

"I sure hope I'm not this complicated when I'm grown up," Thalia said. She put her arms around me.

"Don't worry," I said. "You will be."

"I thought we were just having a good time with good people," Thalia said.

"You were," I said. "Mama wasn't."

"You mean she's jealous?" Thalia said.

"You mean envious," I said. "And no, she's not. But things were a certain way when she left today. She comes back a few hours later and they're different. She's right; we should have left a note. She went looking for us, with no idea where we were, and when she found us, we were in a room full of people she's met once or never, there was drinking going on, and nobody else our age around. See what I mean? She went by what she saw, not by what we know."

"Oh," Thalia said. "I guess I do." She hugged me harder. "Did you have a good time?"

"I guess so," I shrugged. "It sure went by faster than I thought."

"That means you're enjoying yourself, doesn't it?"

"It can."

"Did you notice the way Carlos was looking at you?" Thalia asked.

I stepped out of my sister's embrace.

"Stop trying to make me say I enjoyed myself," I said. "We ended up at a party we didn't expect and we came home again. That's about all that happened. And I do not care what Carlos or anyone else here thinks about me, okay?"

Mama came out of the shower wrapped in a towel.

"I get paid Friday," she said. "It won't be a full week, but it's money. We can buy gas and pay the utilities. If there's anything left over, we can splurge on toilet paper."

She tried to smile. "I'm over being angry at you two for being so thoughtless," she said. "Just don't ever go off without telling me where you're going again."

"No, Mama," Thalia said.

And I thought, *What are you going to do if I do? Ship me off to Mississippi?* But I didn't say it.

"Elektra?" Mama said.

"Sure."

"God, it's almost one in the morning," Mama said. "Let's go to bed."

The big brass bed that filled our tiny bedroom creaked a little as I slid in. Tonight, Thalia was in the middle.

The blankets warmed and I began to feel sort of cozy. It made me remember Carlos's arms around me and how warm they'd been. I felt a little sorry for Mama that she'd missed that evening. She'd have loved to play Rob's silly game, and she'd have taken Carlos's portrait of her and kept it someplace safe. Poor Mama. She'd found what she'd come looking for and she hadn't been there to enjoy it. I'd enjoyed it, but it wasn't what I wanted. Maybe we were both trapped.

A little gray light touched the tarnished brass at the foot of the bed. It looked like a few ribs from some long-dead thing. Their shadow on the door was indefinite, but looked enough like the bars of a cell to make me feel caged.

"Tomorrow, I've got to get more money," I said to myself. "However I do it."

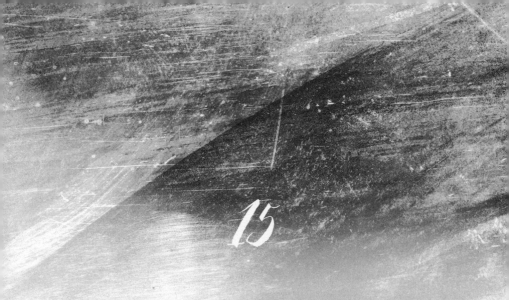

_15_

Early the next morning, there was a slow pounding on the door. It woke me, but I wasn't in a mood to answer it. I was still tired from the previous night, and I resented whoever was interrupting my sleep. Thalia climbed over me and went to answer it instead.

I heard Ralph's thick voice.

"Hi," he said. "How's George?"

"He's just fine, Mr. Ralph," Thalia said. "And how are you today?"

"Can I talk to your mother?"

"She's not up just yet," Thalia said. "May I take a message?"

"No," Ralph said. "I'll just wait here."

"Would you like me to take your gun while you wait?" Thalia said.

"No, thanks," Ralph said. Then he said, "At ease!"

At the word "gun," I was no longer drowsy. "Mama, wake up," I said, giving her a shove and getting out of bed.

Ralph was standing at the door with one hand behind his back and his rifle held out by the muzzle, as if he were on parade. He was wearing a worn gray poncho, ragged jeans, and a pair of tired lace-up boots.

"Good morning," I said.

Ralph didn't say anything.

"Good morning, sir," I said.

A slight nod.

"Can I help you?"

A slight shake of the head.

Then Mama was there in her sweatpants and the T-shirt she slept in.

When he saw her, Ralph sprang to attention. He reached into his pocket and handed her a carefully folded square of white paper.

"Ma'am," Ralph said. "I need you to know that I didn't steal that solenoid. Here's the receipt. In case the solenoid's not the problem and you need to return it. Only your car runs now, so the solenoid was the problem."

Mama didn't take the paper.

"You bought a solenoid for my car?"

A nod.

"Do you mind if I ask why?"

"You needed it," Ralph said.

Mama didn't say anything.

I looked at that rifle, old, black, and ugly. I wondered who it had killed.

Then Thalia pushed past me and Mama and stepped down to Ralph. She gave him a quick hug and a light kiss on the cheek. Then she took the receipt.

"Thank you, Mr. Ralph," she said. "You know, you don't need to bring your gun when you come to call. We'll always be glad to see you."

Ralph took a step back and dropped his rifle in surprise. He raised his hand to the cheek she'd kissed. A snaggletoothed smile flashed across his face.

"Okay!"

Then he bent over, picked up the rifle, put it across his chest, about-faced like the same soldier on parade, and marched away.

I stared at my sister.

"How the hell did you think to do that?"

"It was obvious," Thalia said.

Mama sagged against the doorframe and shook her

head. "Just another quiet morning in California," she said. "Well, I'm up. I have a car that runs. Which means I can go on interviews."

As for me, I was reminded that Ralph had money and that he might be persuaded to part with some of it. How could I manage to transfer some of it from him to me? If I had the money, I could be on my way home now, before things got any worse. Before Daddy did something stupid or desperate.

It was a question that occupied me through breakfast, without giving me any answers. What Would Odysseus Do? Wise, counseling Odysseus, the man of many turnings, the smartest and most cunning of the Greek heroes. Taker of Troy, defeater of the Cyclops—what would he do in this situation?

Probably lie. Anyway, that's what I was going to do.

Okay, so I was going to lie to a nice, kind veteran with PTSD or something, to try to trick him into giving me money for a bus ticket home. That only left the question of what lie I was going to tell him. What lie would work?

"I'm going out," I said. "But I'll be back in a couple of hours."

"Can I come?" Thalia said.

"No."

"Why not?"

"Because I'm going to sell myself over at Alix's to raise money to buy you shoes for school, and I don't want you to know where it comes from."

"Very funny."

"Someone has to do it."

Mama was tapping slowly at her computer.

"See you later," I said.

"I don't want to go with you anyway," I heard Thalia say to the closing door.

I decided to make my way over to Ralph's place and take a closer look at it. It might give me insight into some of the details of his madness, and that might help me with my lie. Up ahead, I saw him heading out on his morning rounds, dragging a flat wooden wagon with thick black tires. No shopping cart for Ralph; he was a professional scavenger.

I couldn't tell what kind of boat Ralph's used to be. The superstructure was gone and had been replaced with a sort of tent made of patched canvas tarps. A fence surrounded it, the only fence anywhere in the marina. It was made of sticks and stakes of different kinds and some rusty barbed wire was looped loosely in and out of them. But there was only one strand, and it didn't run all the way around the fence, so Ralph had pieced it out with some clothesline and a length of chain.

Between the fence and the boat was a collection of junk. A lot of it was stuff I didn't recognize. Some I did. Worn-out tires, oil drums, rotting scraps of jagged plywood, a glassless window frame, a picnic table with no legs at one end, and about a half mile of garden hose were some of the things I knew. The rest were just metal shapes.

Set up next to the bow of the boat, on a base made of one of those shapes, was a wooden statue of a woman. A very unusual woman. For one thing, she was wearing an army helmet. For another, she had a rifle tied crossways on her chest with baling wire. And she had a couple of boards sticking out from her back that I guessed were supposed to be wings.

One more thing about Ralph's place stood out to me: it looked like every seagull on San Francisco Bay had come there to poop. A gull there now, perched on the army helmet. He turned his head from side to side like he was waiting for me to do something.

"What?" I said. "I don't have any food."

"*Awgh*," he said, and went on watching me.

"Are you here for a handout, too?" I said.

The seagull hopped to a different angle and twitched his head again. Then he lifted himself slowly into the air and glided out over the bay.

For the first time, I noticed that the statue had a name. ST. BARBARA had been scratched into the metal base in ragged, unsteady letters.

And under this, just above the mud, in smaller letters: WHEN THE GUNS ARE SILENT THE MUSES ARE HEARD.

The Muses? How had Ralph known about them? In Greece, each one of the arts had its own patron goddess. There were nine of them, including the one my sister was named for: Thalia the Muse of Comedy. But they were eons older than any saint.

The statue looked ugly and unfinished, but there was a crude kind of power in the half-finished face and the skewed wings that reached inside me and made my angry heart wince. There was so much longing in the thing.

I took three tentative steps inside the fence and touched the statue. I had very few opinions about saints, but I had always more or less expected them to be sympathetic to people in need.

"Help me," I said. "Help me home."

Then, feeling like an idiot, I backed out of Ralph's yard and went on my way. I had gotten as much of what I had come for as I was going to get. Now I had to think about how I might use it.

One thing I had decided Guadalupe Slough had going for it: the nearly always empty streets were great for thinking. I walked randomly up and down them, imagining scenarios in which I said something to Ralph that would cause him to say, "Wait here," disappear into his boat, and come back with a fistful of money.

Was I being skeevy? I was. But once I was back where I belonged, I could start being a good person again. I could repay Ralph the money I'd taken, which would make it borrowing. I would explain what I'd had to do to Daddy. I would mention Odysseus. He would give me the money to get me straight again, and if he didn't, I'd get it some other way. It really wasn't that much that I would need.

Don't think about what you have to do, I told myself. *Think about why you're doing it. Once you're back where you belong, you can make everything right again.*

So I imagined several different dramas I could construct.

Hi, Ralph. Listen, my family's having an emergency. Back home in Mississippi. Mama wants to send me back to deal with it, but—well, you know we just got here, and she spent all her money on our place, so I was wondering if you could let me borrow enough for a bus ticket back to Cleburne. My dad can pay you back as soon as I get home.

Not bad, but more detail would be better, more convincing.

Ralph, my father's in the hospital. He says it's not serious, but we think he's trying not to worry us. Mama wants to send me back to check on him, but all our money's tied up in our place right now. Is there any way I can borrow enough for a bus ticket home? Dad can pay you back as soon as I get there.

No, that went too far from the truth. I needed something closer. Something that would make me feel less like the no-good lying sneak I was determined to be.

Ralph, listen. My father's in some kind of trouble back home. He's had a breakdown of some kind. They're telling us not to worry, but that's bullshit. Nobody tells you not to worry unless there's something to worry about. Anyway, Mama wants to send me home to check on him, find out what's really going on. The thing is, all of our money's tied up in our place right now, so I was wondering—could you loan me the money for a bus ticket home? I can pay you back as soon as I get there, but I've got to know what's going on with my father.

I liked this one. It had the virtue of the best lies; it was partly true. In fact, as far as I was concerned, it was almost all true. The only real lie was that Mama wasn't in on my plan. And there was that word *breakdown*. I hoped it would make Ralph sympathetic. Anyway, that was the one I was going to go with. As for paying him back, of course I would. I would. But I had to get back to Mississippi.

16

The only problem was, Ralph didn't come home. I hung around in front of his place until an hour after dark. Then I gave up. The angular, weird statue of St. Barbara or whatever it was was beginning to creep me out anyway. In the dark, its shadow looked very judgmental. I decided it didn't approve of my plans or even want to help me get home.

Home. Had anyone called me back? I checked. No, they hadn't. What the hell was up with my friends? Had they forgotten how to use a phone? Never mind, I'd give them a good blessing-out when I got back.

With one last look over my shoulder, I took in the statue, the rattling reeds, and the almost silent sea beyond them, and then I went back home . . . no—back to where I was going to sleep that night.

When I got there, Mama, Rob, and Thalia were sitting in our living room. There was a pizza the size of a truck tire on the dinette table and a bottle of wine beside it. Mama had her feet up and a glass in her hand. Rob was scribbling in a notebook while Thalia and Mama threw words at him.

"Railroad."

"Epiphany."

"Turtle."

Rob put his hand over his eyes while Thalia announced the time in ten-second increments. Just after she said "Seventy seconds," he announced,

"Turtle on the tracks

Epiphany of slowness.

Railroad ran here once."

"Yay, that's seventeen," Thalia said.

"My God that's the worst one yet," Mama said. And giggled.

"I promise you, that's nothing compared to how bad I can be," Rob said. He took a sip from his own glass.

"Why aren't you at work?" I asked.

"It's been very eventful around here since you left," Mama said.

"As soon as you walked out the door, things started to happen," Thalia said. "Wait'll you hear."

"First of all, I'm not washing dishes because when I showed up to work, there'd been a grease fire in the kitchen, and the restaurant is closed for a day or two," Mama said. "Secondly, I am drinking wine with this wonderful friend and terrible poet because we are celebrating."

"Celebrating what?"

"I called a former client," Rob said, "the headmaster at the Moore-Windham School, to tell him about your mother. Just to see if there were any positions there. Mike said they had a combination English–Creative Writing gig coming open this fall, and an immediate need for someone to help out in their day care program. Anyway, Helen has an interview tomorrow at eleven. So, we're celebrating."

"What's the Moore-Windham School?"

"The oldest and poshest private school in this end of the bay," Rob said. "They pay like a state university."

"Well swell," I said. "But shouldn't you wait to celebrate until after you've got the job?"

"Elektra, they called as soon as Rob hung up. They asked when I could start at the day care. I interview tomorrow. Tonight we are celebrating that," Mama said. "If I get the teaching job, we'll celebrate that, too."

"I don't mean to be negative or anything, but what if you don't?" I said.

"Then we'll celebrate something else," Thalia said.

"Sometimes when you jump blind, life catches you," Mama said.

"What about you," Rob said. "Any adventures to report?"

"No," I said. "I just took in the richly exotic atmosphere of this place. Again. I went by Ralph's, but he wasn't home. That's my day." I went over and pulled off a slice of pizza. "Do you think he's all right?" I said, as casually as I could.

"Yeah," Rob said. "Sometimes he goes off for a few days on long-range penetration missions. Then he comes back, usually with something special he's been looking for, sleeps for a day or two, and goes back to his routine. He came back with a parachute once."

Well, that was unwelcome news. I was marooned until Ralph came back. WWOD?

Whatever the answer to that was, I had a situation in front of me to deal with.

It was clear as the light on Olympus that Mama and Rob were flirting. That was bad enough, in front of Thalia and me for God's sake, but they were doing it by pretending to argue about writing.

"You're wasting your time playing around with haikus," Mama said. "You should be writing real poems. True haiku aren't even possible in English."

"One of the most important uses of time is to waste it," Rob said. "I'm surprised you still haven't learned that. Don't you know how to waste time when you're writing?"

"When I write, I'm trying as hard as I can to concentrate," Mama said.

"Well, maybe that's your problem," Rob said. "When I write—when I really sit down to write—I expect to spend about half of my time fooling around with pencils or looking up junk on my computer."

"Well, maybe it's because I've never had all day to spend on my work," Mama said. "I couldn't just walk away from taking care of my family and live on a boat in the reeds."

"Emily Brontë ran the whole house," Rob said. "Took care of her crazy brother and father and still got her work done. Emily Dickinson, too."

"Just change your name to Emily," I suggested.

"And, Mama, now you are living on a boat in some reeds," Thalia pointed out.

"You're all attacking me," Mama said. Then she poured another glass of wine. "And you're just doing it because I want to see something accomplished at the end of the day. Something good on paper."

"Exactly," Rob said. "A lot of things take more than one day to see any results."

"Says the man who was going to kill himself a few days ago because he hadn't published anything in five years," Mama said.

"And wouldn't that have been a mistake?" Rob said. "I thought I'd wasted the last five years. Turns out I hadn't."

"Maybe you did," Mama said. "The jury's still out."

"Not guilty, Your Honor," Rob said.

I wanted to scream. Mama wasn't even divorced yet, and maybe she wasn't ever going to be. I bet she didn't even care about Rob. She just wanted to play writer.

Why hadn't Ralph come home tonight?

Then, like magic, or maybe like fate, someone knocked on the door.

When I opened it, there was Ralph.

"Hi," he said. "Brought you something."

There, on his wagon, was a cast-iron stove about the size of a microwave oven.

"Thought it might come in handy this winter," he said.

"Why thank you, Ralph, I suppose it might," I said.

"Mama, come see what Ralph has brought us."

Mama, Thalia, and Rob all clustered in the doorway.

"Amazing," Rob said. He sounded a little slurred from the wine.

"Where did you get this?" Mama asked.

"Put it in my head and went till I found it," Ralph explained.

"But it doesn't have a stovepipe," Thalia said.

"That'll be easy," Ralph said. Then he lifted the stove off his wagon, carried it up the saggy ramp, and put it down on our deck.

"Well. Thank you," Mama said. "It's very nice of you, Ralph. But please don't bring us anything more for a while. We have a very small place."

"Wanted to talk to you, too," Ralph said, looking at me. "Wanted to talk about that dancing."

"The dervish dance?"

"Yeah," Ralph said. "You give lessons?"

WWOD?

"Let's talk about that," I said. "Come on in."

So Ralph joined us, and the whole evening changed direction—this time in my direction. Mama and Rob stopped flirting, and Thalia and I made a fuss over Ralph. Thalia, bless her, because she really cared about his adventures in quest of junk, and I because of the reasons you already know.

I didn't give him an answer about dance lessons right away. But after Ralph and Rob and Mama had finished the wine and Rob had done three more haikus, each worse than the last, and he had gone, I told Ralph I would teach him what I knew and we'd talk about price later.

Then I said I'd walk over to his place with him and announced that I'd be right back.

"Be right back," Mama said, like I hadn't said it.

"I'm coming, too," Thalia said.

"No, you're not," I said.

"Mean," Thalia said, but for a wonder she didn't try to tag along, maybe because it would have looked like trying to tag along.

"I'm really glad you came by tonight," I said to Ralph once we were outside. Which was true enough. "I was getting pretty tired of watching Rob and Mama murder poetry." Which was also true enough. Then I ducked my head and lowered my voice and said, "Actually, there's something I have to ask you . . ." and I told the lie.

I have to say, it went over well with Ralph. He didn't even ask what the trouble was, or anything else I hadn't thought to make up. All he said was, "How much do you need?" and "When will you be back?"

To which I said, "Just a few hundred" and "As soon as I can."

Then he said, "Wait here," and went into his boat. I waited, avoiding eye contact with the statue, which I was sure was frowning down on me.

In a few minutes, he came back with a small paper bag. "There's about three hundred," he said.

"Oh, Ralph," I said. "You've saved us. I really think you have." And then, because part of me felt really rotten at cheating and lying to him, I said, "Let's dance right now."

"Thanks," he said, and there in the gray darkness on the street, in front of the statue that was his saint and muse and who knew what else, we did. I danced until my ankle started hurting again, and then I kept on dancing, twirling and twirling with one hand raised to heaven and the other trying to reach the earth. Ralph seemed serene when he did it, and I felt like I owed him something.

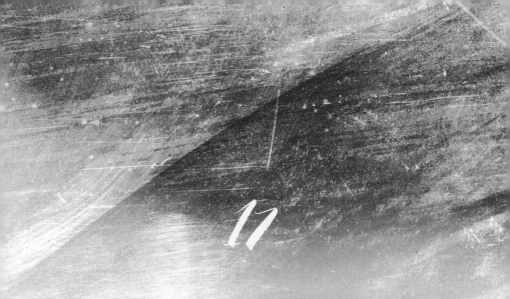

17

Mama was angry when I got home.

"You said you'd be right back," she said.

"He wanted to dance. It helps him," I said.

My money was tucked inside my shirt. I needed a place to stash it until morning. My plan was to wait until Mama went to her interview, then gently segue out the door with some excuse to Thalia, and get myself any way I could to the bus station. To avoid suspicion, I'd take nothing with me. I had enough money from Ralph to buy a toothbrush and food and whatever else I might need for a day or two. Then I'd be home and I wouldn't need anything. And I could start making everything right. For Daddy, for Ralph, and even for me.

But where could I put the money until then?

I solved problem one by flouncing out onto the deck as

though I were angry, and quietly, quietly opening the door to the cast-iron stove.

"See you tomorrow," I whispered to my money, my way back to Mississippi. Then I hung around outside for a few minutes until I got chilled by the wind.

When I went back in, Mama and I had a short fight about my unreliability, but I wasn't really interested in my side of it, as I figured it was the last one I was going to have for a while. It died out after a few minutes, and we all sat around in the kind of heavy weather that back home means a thunderstorm is coming.

I took out my phone to check the address of the bus station. To my total lack of surprise, it was miles away in downtown San José and to walk to it would probably take me half a day. I scoped out a couple of local buses that would get me there in an hour or two. Of course, neither one ran to Guadalupe Slough, but one had a stop a mile or so away across the highway. Good enough.

"What are you doing?" Thalia said, figuring the heavy weather had gone on long enough.

"Playing a game," I said.

"You don't play games," she said.

I put my phone away.

"You're right, they're stupid."

I fished a book out of one of the boxes in the corner and pretended to read. I had to pretend pretty hard, as it turned out to be one of my mother's books on writing. I had opened it randomly to the chapter on character development. Fascinating topic. I kept staring at the words.

Your characters are defined by their actions, no matter how small they may seem. Mrs. Dalloway decides to buy the flowers herself. Hamlet decides to talk to the ghost. Frodo takes the ring. All of these are choices, none is inevitable. All lead to other choices that would not have to be made had the first choice not been what it was. And so you go through your story, choice by choice, until you come to the end, whatever that is.

There was a lot more of it. But that paragraph really got my back up. It made it sound like choices were easy, automatic and clean. Like hell they were. Mama's choice to drag us out here had been just short of bloody. And it was forcing me to do things I would never have done if we'd stayed home where we belonged. And what choices did we have, anyway?

In stories, there's always a right choice. What if you're in a story where there is no right choice, then what? And what if you don't even know what all of your choices are?

I was so angry at that stupid book, I wanted to throw it across the room. But that, of course, would have meant another pointless fight with Mama.

Instead, I decided to play nice with Thalia.

I pushed out my unhurt foot and nudged her. Her head came up out of her game.

"Hey, wart, let's do something," I said.

"Like what?" Thalia said.

"Name it," I said.

"Thirty-one," she said. "Mama, would you like to play Thirty-one with us?"

Mama had brought one nice outfit with her from Mississippi. It was a standard little black dress suit and a pale lavender silk blend blouse. She was ironing it, using the table as a board.

"Maybe when I'm done here, if it isn't too late," she said.

"Let's see how you look," I said. No reason not to spread the nice around a little.

So, when she had finished the dress, she went into the bedroom and put it on. She came out and turned around for us, and it looked exactly the way it had in Mississippi, but Thalia and I acted like we'd never seen it before. I think it cheered her up.

"God, I'm so nervous," she said.

"You'll do fine, Mama," Thalia said.

"Besides, this guy is a friend of Rob's," I said. "I'll bet you've already got it on that basis."

"But what if I get lost and I'm late?" Mama said. "What if I can't even find the place? You know how I drive."

"Leave an hour early to give yourself plenty of time for it," I said. "Then maybe the universe won't be interested in screwing you up."

She laughed and then went and changed. Thalia got out a deck of cards and the three of us played Thirty-one for a while.

But the universe, or fate, or the gods, or maybe just bloody, unplotted life was just waiting for the sun to come up and mess with all of us.

18

Mama took my advice. Her interview was at eleven. She was out the door before ten. I heard the growly little engine of the bug start up and grind away toward downtown San José, and I got out of bed.

I'd been pretending to be drowsy. The truth was, I was just waiting for her to get the hell out of Guadalupe Slough so I could get going.

Thalia was already up, sitting by the front door. Boozer had come by on his morning rounds and was lying on his back wagging his tail while Thalia rubbed his belly and crooned, "Good boy, good boy, good Boozer dog," over and over again, sentiments with which Boozer appeared to agree completely.

"That was nice last night," she said.

"Yeah," I said. "Do you need the bathroom? I want to shower."

She didn't, so I did. While I was trying to pretend that the tepid little stream was, in fact, a satisfying shower, it crossed my mind that I should call Daddy and give him a heads-up that I was coming. He'd want to meet me at the station in Cleburne, no matter what he'd said about what was best for me and Thalia.

As soon as I was dressed, I called.

"The number you have dialed has been disconnected, and there is no new number. If you feel you have reached this recording in error—"

I looked at my phone. I had hit redial on my most recent call home. The number had to be right. I hit it again.

"The number you have dialed has been—"

Okay, okay. I dialed it by hand.

"The number you have dialed—"

What the fuck was going on? Why had Daddy disconnected my only lifeline to him? Whatever was going on, I wasn't going to be able to do anything about it here. I had to get going.

I took my two ten-dollar bills from their hiding place under the drawer. Then I checked the refrigerator, but it was nearly empty. We'd run through all of the snacks, too. No problem. I'd eat when I got to the bus station. I had plenty of money for a two- or three-day trip.

The money. Which was still in the cast-iron stove, on the deck, next to Thalia.

I went back out. Sure enough, Thalia was still there. Now she was lying down by Boozer with her arm around him, looking up at the sky and lazily rubbing one of his ears.

"Every town should have a town dog," she said.

"It's a shame we don't have any food for him," I said.

"Yeah," Thalia said. "I wonder who feeds him? I bet Erik does. I bet that's why Boozer spends so much time at the library."

I reached into my pocket and pulled out ten dollars.

"Why don't you go over to the Mercado and see what you can get for Boozer with this?" I said.

"Huh?" Thalia said. "Why are you being nice all of a sudden?"

"Do you want it or not?" I said.

Thalia got up. So did Boozer.

"We want it," she said. "But we're real surprised."

"Maybe this is one of those moments of wonder that Rob is always trying to have," I said.

"It must be," Thalia said. "'Cause I sure wonder why you're doing it."

"Thank you very much," I said.

"Thank *you* very much," Thalia said. "On Boozer's behalf. Come on, boy."

Down the street they went, a girl and her dog. As soon as they turned the corner, I rescued my cash. It looked lovely sitting there in the little paper bag, like it was happy and excited to be spent.

"Come on," I said to it. "Let's go."

As I walked away, it occurred to me for the first time that I should have left a note. But now that would mean going back, and maybe getting caught by Thalia. I'd call from the road tonight. I wouldn't say where I was or where I was going; I'd just tell them not to worry and ask how Mama's interview had gone.

I reached the highway that cut off Guadalupe Slough from the rest of San José. It was packed with cars, and they were moving fast. Maybe a mile away, I could see a crosswalk under a cluster of traffic lights. I'd have to backtrack to get to the bus stop, but there was no way I was going to try to dash across six lanes of traffic. By the time I got across, I was nearly an hour into my trip. And I was starting to get hungry.

Following the directions on my phone, I found a small green and white bus stop sign on a lamppost. The number on the sign said this was the bus I wanted, so I waited. I waited almost another hour. It turned out that the previous bus had broken down, and the bus that finally arrived was carrying all that bus's passengers as well as its own. I found one square foot of space and felt it shrinking around the edges as we moved deeper into San José.

By the time we go to my transfer point, I was sweating.

At least the second bus was only ten minutes late and carrying a normal complement of passengers. It was almost luxurious, until, about halfway through the ride, a tall, rangy man with scraggly brown hair got on, loomed over our driver, and asked in a voice like a grizzy's growl, "Is this a good day to visit religious SHRINES?"

"Well, there's St. Joseph's Cathedral," the driver said. "We go almost right past it. And there's the Buddhist temple over by Overfelt Park—"

"I was asking you about the WEATHER," the man said, walking down the aisle. He stopped a few feet away and then sat down next to me.

No, no, no, no, no, no, no, no . . .

That was what I kept saying over and over in my head, while the man hummed a tune that sounded like a duet between a rusty saw and a carsick cat.

When he had gotten the tune just right, he turned to me and said, "Do you like GOD?"

My eyes were closed, and my arms were crossed over my torso. Maybe I looked dead to him, hence the question. He might have thought that I had just had my interview with Him.

"Do you like GOD?" the man said again.

Into my endless loop of noes came some of the few words I knew in Ancient Greek, from the opening of *The Iliad*, words Daddy had used as a sort of lullaby when I was little. I'd learned the sounds without having a clue what they meant. I turned to the man and said, "Sing, Muse of the wrath of Pelleas's son Achilleus." In my best Classical Greek.

The man just stared at me.

"You Mexican?" he said finally.

"Sing, Muse of the wrath of Pelleas's son Achilleus." I remembered another bit, and added, "No man or woman, born coward or brave, can shun his destiny."

He got up and moved to another seat.

"She's CRAZY," he told the bus driver when he got off at the next stop.

The rest of my trip was uneventful.

My bus finally stopped in front of the main San José terminal, and I went inside.

It was a mix of old linoleum, old paint, old pinball games, and a smell of cleanser. I found a ticket window and bought a one-way to Cleburne. Because of my first bus's breakdown, I had missed the morning bus out, so I'd have to wait for the four o'clock. But I had my ticket, I was here, and that meant I was on the way home. What else did I need? I'd be home in two days, and then I'd sort everything out.

I hit the cafeteria and treated myself to a breakfast of plastic eggs and cardboard toast. I played pinball on one of the machines. As I waited for my bus, I looked around at all the people—so many more different kinds of people than you'd see in Cleburne—and thought how lost they looked and wondered where they were going.

I checked the square silver clock hanging from the ceiling. 12:07 it said. 12:08.

If Mama had gotten to her interview, it was over by now. I was sure she'd snagged the day care job. The teaching gig would be harder to get, but I felt pretty sure she would. Mama was kind of brilliant in her own way, and she loved to talk about English.

12:21, 12:22 . . . 1:17, 1:18

God, waiting was hard. I just wanted to get on the bus and find myself immediately at home. Was that too much to ask?

I imagined how it was going to be when I got home. I was supposed to get into Cleburne a little before three in the afternoon. I wouldn't call Daddy. I'd get a ride from one of my friends or walk home from the bus station if I had to. Then I'd let myself into the house, and if he wasn't there, I'd just move back into my room and wait for him. If he was there, I'd throw my arms around him and tell him everything was going to be all right. That made me smile.

I noticed the sun had burned off most the clouds, and people on the other side of the glass doors were getting on and off the buses in a gray-yellow light. I decided to take a walk around the block, just in case anyone back home ever asked me what San José was like.

That took about five minutes.

I tried calling Daddy again. This had the same results as before. Where was he, and why was he doing this?

1:53, 1:54.

I thought about calling Tracy and letting her know I was coming, asking her if she knew anything about Daddy.

But that wasn't good. If I did that, it would be all over campus that Professor Kamenides was not only separated from his wife, but his children didn't even know what he was doing. That was not going to get out there if I could help it.

Then I thought of a way I could do it. I could tell Tracy I was coming home for a visit. Brilliant. I took out my phone.

Hey, GF. Can U pick me up at the bus stn in 2 days? Coming home. Don't tell my dad. It's a surprise. PS Cali is way kewl.

There, that ought to get me an answer. At the least she'd have to text me back to tell me she couldn't do it.

1:23, 1:24, 1:25.

My phone buzzed.

Oh hi Elektra. So sorry about yr Dad.

My thumb rapped back, *No prob. I'm coming bk to deal with it. Update me.*

I had to wait half an hour for an answer then I got: *What can u do about it?*

Again, I typed, *UPDATE.*

U knew he resigned, right?

NO.

Yesterday. No, day b4. Movers came 2day.

Okay, now I was scared. Scared enough to stop pretending that I knew what was going on. I typed, *Where did he go?*

??????? was her answer.

Texting was taking too long. I called her.

"Oh, hi, Elektra," was all Tracy said when she answered.

"Tracy, tell me," I said. "Pretend I don't know anything. Tell me everything you heard."

There was a pause. Then she said, "Well, you know about his other wife, right?"

"What?" I said. "That's crazy, Tracy. My father was never married before."

"Not before," Tracy told me. "Since."

19

I was so dizzy my head felt like it was trying to detach from my neck. I was shaking.

"Tracy," I said. "That's crazy. Is that what they're saying back home?"

"They're saying it because it's true," Tracy said. "Look, I shouldn't have to be the one telling you this. I mean, your mother knew. She must have known, right?"

"No. She couldn't have. I don't know. Tracy, tell me where he is now," I said.

"He's with her, wherever they went," Tracy said. "I don't know any more than I'm telling you. I'm sorry, Elektra, but I just don't."

There was dead air between us. I hung in it, not knowing what to say, or what to ask, or anything. At that moment, I wasn't completely sure of who I was.

Finally Tracy said, "Elektra, my mom is calling me. I have to go."

I nodded and hung up.

I sat in my plastic bucket chair, staring into the old brown linoleum. Around me, the lost-looking people flowed through the terminal. I was one of them now.

Daddy was married to someone else. Daddy was married to Mama. When had this happened? Years ago? Last week? Was this why Mama had dragged us out to the car in such a hurry? Was this why Daddy hadn't tried to stop her? Was this why my friends had stopped answering my messages?

I had to admit it probably was. Nothing right, tight little Cleburne cherished more than a good scandal, and the story of the famous professor with two wives would grow and spread like a campus oak. It would be there for a hundred years, casting shade on us. And my good friends wouldn't want to be associated with someone who was part of it. We were all snobs, and, unlike me, they were from old Cleburne families.

Scandal. It was a word I'd never used in my life. A supermarket checkout counter word. You saw it staring at you and bought some scandal along with your milk and canned goods. Now it was part of my life, and I hadn't even done anything. I hadn't even known about it. I hated Daddy for doing it to me. I hated Mama for not telling us. I hated my friends for abandoning me.

After a while, I went into the women's room and vomited. When I came out, I checked the silver clock.

2:06.

Well, going to Mississippi was no longer on my agenda. I might as well go back to Slip 19 and confront Mama with what I knew. I decided to call Thalia and let her know where I was. She was the only person I wasn't furious with.

I had four missed calls and one new message.

"Elektra, where are you? I need you to get back here," Thalia's voice said. "Mama's hurt bad. She's in the hospital. Call me back, please."

I called Thalia back.

"Where are you?" she wailed.

"Where's Mama?" I said. "What happened?"

"Mama had her interview. She got the day care job. Then she got lost on the way home. She turned the wrong way down a one-way street and some guy in a pickup smashed into her. Where are you?" she wailed again.

"How bad is she?" I said.

"They won't let me see her," Thalia said.

Then there was a new voice on the phone.

"Hi, Elektra, this is Rob. I'm with Thalia. Your mom's in bad shape, but she's going to be fine. As soon as she's out of intensive care, you'll be able to see her. The car's totaled, but you have to expect that. And the other guy turns out to have been high, so that's to her advantage legally . . . Sorry, I still think like a lawyer, you know? Anyway, we'll just have to take it one step at a time today, right?"

"Is my mama really going to be okay?" I said. "You can tell me."

"Yes," Rob said.

"How do you know?"

"T'Pring is friends with one of the nurses at County General," Rob said. "She asked her to find out anything she could. Your mother had her leg and some ribs broken. Oh, and one arm. But she also had her pelvis broken, and that's a lot more serious. But it's all bones, you know? Nothing that can't heal up in a few months."

I could hear Thalia crying in the background.

"She's still in surgery," Rob went on. "As soon as she can have visitors, I'll take you guys down to see her. Where are you, anyway?"

"I'm coming," I said. "But it's going to take me a while to get there. Can I talk to Thalia, please?"

"Of course."

"Oh, wait. Rob?"

"Yes?"

"Thank you."

"You're welcome," Rob said. "Here's Thalia."

"Thalia," I said.

"Yeah. Where are you?"

"It doesn't matter," I said. "No, wait. That's not fair. I'm at the bus station. I was going to take a bus back to Mississippi and straighten everything out. But that's not going to happen. . . . I don't know what's going to happen now. The only thing I do know is we've got each other and nobody else. I'm coming back, and I'm never going to run out on you again."

"Just get yourself home," she said.

Heading back to the slough on the bus only took about an hour. By the time I got there, the afternoon wind was coming up, and it wasn't gentle. I could feel grit in it, blowing into my eyes.

Boozer was wandering down the street looking for a place to get out of the blast. He whined when he saw me coming, wagged his tail, and joined me.

"Oh, come on in," I told him. "Maybe you can cheer up Thalia a little."

We'd never had a dog or cat. Daddy didn't care about pets, and Mama didn't want the extra work. We'd had a couple of goldfish once and an iguana that ran off when Thalia took it outside for a walk, but that was all. Now I was breaking one of the Laws of Kamenides, letting a dog in the house. But who was there to tell me I couldn't? And anyway, Boozer wasn't a pet, he was just another citizen of the slough.

"Come on," I said again.

Boozer looked at me like it was about time somebody had done the decent thing and followed me through the door.

Rob and Thalia were sitting on the sofa staring at the wall.

"Any more news?" I asked.

Boozer headed right over to Thalia and put his head on her knee. That dog knew how to play a sucker. Thalia bent her head over his and wept.

"Your mother's out of surgery," Rob said. "She'll be in intensive care for a while. Nobody can say how long. A few days, anyway."

I sat down at the kitchen table. Now that I was back, everything that had happened today suddenly weighed even more than it had before, a lot more. What were we going to do?

WWOD? Who cared? Odysseus had been a man in a man's world and he hadn't had a little sister to look out for or a mother in the hospital. He'd been alone, isolated from everyone he cared about, and that had made him free. I wasn't. The future looked black as Hades. But it was the only future I had.

"Don't try to decide anything tonight," Rob said, as if he'd been reading my thoughts. "It's too soon. You don't even know what you're dealing with. Tomorrow, things will be a little clearer."

"Tomorrow things will be just like they are today," I said. "Unless they get worse."

"One thing we should do is get in touch with your father," Rob said. "Unless you've already done that. Have you?"

That was when I started to cry.

When I could talk again, I told Rob and Thalia what I'd found out.

Thalia cried harder.

Rob came over and sat down across from me and put his hand on my shoulder.

"Two things," he said. "One, you're not alone here. It just feels that way. And two, speaking as your attorney, you couldn't have given me better news."

"You're not our attorney," I said. "Anyway, we can't pay you."

"You saved my life, remember?" Rob said.

There was a knock on the door.

"I'll get it," Rob said.

I could hear Maizie and Alix's voices.

"How is she? Any news? How are the kids?"

This last question didn't seem to need an answer since both the kids were still crying off and on, and at that moment we were pretty loud. Rob spoke with the ladies briefly, then closed the door and came back with a carton full of things from the restaurant.

"I can't eat," I said.

"Me neither," Thalia said.

"Well, let's eat anyway," Rob said. "Food won't fix everything, but just try living without it."

So we did. It was going to be a long night, and I had to admit, even in Hades, Alix's food tasted amazing.

After he'd washed what dishes there were, Rob left, telling us to be sure to come over if we needed anything.

I was as weary as if I'd walked a thousand miles.

"Come on, kid, let's go to bed," I said.

"Can Boozer stay over?" Thalia asked.

"Sure, why not?"

When we went to bed, Boozer followed us. He lay down nearby. Then, when he'd waited what he thought was a decent interval, he climbed up with us.

"Thank you, Boozer," Thalia said.

Boozer rolled over on his back, feet in the air. He let out a long, satisfied grunt.

In the dark, Thalia said, "How long do you think Daddy has had two wives?"

"No idea," I said.

"I think it must have been before we went to Greece," she said. "We kept meeting all those Greek men who wouldn't talk to Mama, and only spoke in Greek. I bet they knew."

"What I wonder is when Mama found out."

"Probably about ten seconds before she packed up her car and threw us into it," Thalia said. She started to cry again. I put an arm around her.

"Mama and Daddy are so damn mean to each other," she said. "You too. Why? What do you get out of it? You make me do all the work of trying to keep us together, and I shouldn't have to. I'm just a kid."

"Is that what you've been doing all this time?" I said. "I thought you just didn't have enough sense to be angry."

"Elektra, you are one stupid big dumb jerk and a pain in the ass."

"Yeah, maybe," I said. "But at least I have you."

20

We finally got to see Mama late the next day.

It was a shock to see her with her legs in the air and covered with whatever they use these days to put broken legs in. And her face looked like a relief map of hell, swollen and colored red, yellow, and blue.

And it didn't help that she cried as soon as she saw us.

"Girls, I'm so sorry," she said. "I had that damned job, and I drove out of that parking lot and in two minutes I didn't know where I was and couldn't even find my way back to the school. Can you fucking believe that?"

"Mama, don't," Thalia said. "It's okay, it's gonna be okay."

I took the hand that didn't have a cast on it.

"Mama, don't worry. Thalia's right," I said. "We got this one. Everybody at the slough has been helping us. You just get well and we'll sort this all out."

She closed her eyes. Didn't say anything. Just squeezed my hand like she was hanging over a cliff.

We stayed with Mama until she started to talk disconnectedly and drowsed off. Then we joined Rob in the waiting room.

"How's she doing?" he asked.

"She'll be fine, but God knows when," I said.

He drove us back to Guadalupe Slough. Since County General was at the south end of town and the slough was at the north, it took almost an hour. It gave me a long time to think.

The main thing we needed was money. Money to keep us going while everything else sorted itself out. Daddy would turn up soon at some new college, and we'd hit him then with the fact that he still had two daughters whether he wanted them or not. Mama would get well. Everything else would unfold as it would. I had to figure out how to keep us in cash somehow while these things happened. It felt better, being able to pare everything down to one problem, even if I didn't have a clue about how to solve it.

When we got back, Mr. Gonzales was sitting on our deck. He looked incomplete without his baseball bat, but his T-shirt was kind of intriguing. It said,

I'D FIND YOU MORE INTERESTING

IF YOU WERE DEAD.

"Wonder what he wants?" I said.

"Don't worry about it," Rob said. "If he gives you any trouble, you know where to come, right?"

"Besides, he's really a pussycat. Carlos says so," Thalia said.

The pussycat raised one hand halfway off his knee when Rob got out of his car. Rob waved back effusively, shouted, "Hi, Mr. Gonzales," and went into his boat.

Thalia and I went up the little ramp that led to our place.

"How's your mama?" Mr. Gonzales asked.

"She'll be okay," I said. "Thanks for asking."

"T'Pring told me it looks like she's gonna be in the hospital for a while," he said.

"Yes," I nodded.

Mr. Gonzales blew out his breath in a long sigh and said, "Okay, here's the deal. You know I own the Mercado, right? Well, anything you need, like toothpaste or groceries or whatever, you just go over there and get it. We'll settle up later. Okay? It's not charity. I don't do charity. You're gonna owe me every cent, okay? But don't worry about that; we'll work it out. Just don't go crazy, okay? And don't tell anybody. Do not ever tell anybody. You tell anybody . . ."

"Mr. Gonzales, not only will we never tell anybody, but if anybody else, one of your employees or someone in your family says you did it, Thalia and I will both swear that they're lying," I said.

And Thalia added, "Nobody's ever going to find out from us that you're the nicest man in the world."

"Okay then," Mr. Gonzales said. He started down the walkway and then jumped into the reeds. Then he turned back.

"You see all this?" he said, taking in the slough with a wave of his arm. "Used to belong to my family. Eight, nine generations back, my ancestor was a soldier in the Spanish army. A *soldado de cuero*, what they called a leather soldier. They were cavalry. Tough men. Anyway, he reached retirement and they gave him a land grant. That's why they founded San José, as a retirement program for the soldiers. But my ancestor, he didn't like his land. Didn't want to farm wheat. So he swapped it for this and became a fisherman. Founded this place. It was all ours. Then the gringos showed up and we lost almost all of it in crooked land deals. So I'm not real crazy about white people. But you're Greeks so I guess that's a little different. Anyway, take care."

And he walked off.

"I think that was the nicest thing anybody's ever done for us," Thalia said. "But I'm not sure, because so many people have been nice to us."

"It sure was," I said. "But I don't want to owe Mr. Gonzales a cent. I want to pay him cash up front for everything we get at his store. Then he'll respect us. I want him to respect us."

"Okay, but how are we going to get money?" Thalia said.

"I don't know, but we'll figure it out."

Then I remembered I had money. I had almost all the money Ralph had given me. But I wasn't going to spend another cent of it. I'd get it back to him and find a way to pay him the rest. I wanted his respect, too.

And, I realized, I wanted to respect myself. I wanted to get started on that right away.

"We're going to be here a while," I said. "We'd better start acting like it. Before we do anything else, let's try to clean the place up. That'll tell us some of the things we need to get. Laundry soap, for instance. We haven't done laundry since we got here."

It felt like I was taking control of my life by stripping the sheets and scouring the sink. And the place was so small, anything we did to make things better felt like a huge improvement. We had to keep running next door to borrow from Rob the things that we'd used to clean his kitchen, and that told us what we'd have to get at the Mercado. By dark, the place looked and felt—not great, but like it was ours. And that was huge.

That left the matter of the laundry, though. Rob had one of those little machines with the dryer on top of the washer, but with just one machine it would take all night to wash our clothes, plus the sheets, plus the blankets. And I was determined to do it all. Just because life was chaotic didn't mean we couldn't have clean sheets. In fact, it made them more important.

According to Rob, there was a tiny laundromat at the back of the Mercado, really a part of it. It was tiny indeed, so small neither of us had noticed it before. Six washers, six dryers, six of those big-wheeled baskets, and no place to sit. When we went there with our things, it was empty. So I got the ten dollars I had left of the money I'd actually earned changed into quarters and put everything in at once. While it was washing, we went back to the Mercado and picked out more house cleaning supplies, along with a very few groceries. That wiped out my honest cash and most of what money Thalia had.

It occurred to me that I had left the bus depot without cashing in my ticket. Too late now, I reckoned. That bus had left the station hours earlier. It gave me a pang to think of the money wasted, but I pushed it down. Time to think of the present—the present, the immediate moment, and whatever chances it offered.

Laundry, laundry, warm water, warm air, and old familiar clothes at the end, clean, folded, and fluffy. It gave me comfort, a sense of some order in the universe. And as I looked at my neatly folded jeans and T-shirts, it gave me something more, though I can't tell you why. It made me feel connected, for just a minute, to the place where I was.

We walked back home in the last twilight, and a few late swallows passed overhead, heading for their nests at the ruined cannery at the end of town. I had all our laundry in a new basket, and Thalia carried a bag of cleaning stuff in one hand and balanced a mop and a broom on her shoulder with the other.

"You know, in its own very weird way, this is kind of a pretty place," I said.

"I know," Thalia said. "I hope we can stay."

"Where else can we go?" I said.

"I don't know, but I don't want to find out," Thalia said. "This is the best place I've ever been."

"Even better than home?"

"I never fit in as well in Mississippi as the rest of y'all," Thalia said. "I always felt like I belonged someplace else. And now we're here and I think this might be it."

"You always fit in," I said. "Little Miss Sunshine from the time you could talk."

"Maybe," Thalia said. "But I never felt like I was the same, and Mississippi likes things to be the same. The first time I ever felt like I was home was that party at Rob's when I sang."

"Wow," I said. "What made the difference?"

"Just that nobody expected me to be a certain way. They didn't expect anybody to be anything but what they were."

"That's true enough," I said. "Which is a good thing when you've got people who are so very unexpectable."

Boozer was waiting for us, lying across our door. When we approached, he got up and wagged his tail and gave Thalia one *woof*.

"Can we—?" Thalia said.

"I guess so," I said. "But I wonder where he slept before we showed up."

"Probably all alone in some horrible place."

"Yeah, he looks totally neglected," I said. "Have you ever noticed he wears a flea collar? I mean, somebody's taking care of him. He's just a bum who likes to hang out."

"Then I'm glad he likes to hang out with us," Thalia said. "I always wanted a dog."

"You do not have a dog," I said. "But I'm pretty sure that a dog has you."

"Yep," Thalia said.

Boozer curled up in a corner while we made the bed and put things away as well as we could. When we had dinner, he stood by the table and stared at us, trying to force us to give him food with the powers of his mind. In Thalia's case, it worked. She made him a plate and put it in the corner of the kitchen.

When he'd eaten, Boozer sauntered into the bedroom and curled up on the fresh blankets. Thalia went in to join him. I could hear her soft "Good boys" and his happy snuffs coming through the doorway.

I was left alone, which was just what I wanted to be for the moment. Alone to see where I was.

Tectonic.

The word came up from somewhere, and I rolled it on my tongue. Tectonic. From the Greek *tekton*, which means "builder."

The world floats on huge islands of rock riding on a molten sea, and those islands are called tectonic plates. Probably because everything in our world is built on them. Two of them come together here in California, and that's why there are so many earthquakes here. The earth shifts underfoot. I'd had two earthquakes today, and, boy howdy, the earth had sure shifted. My daddy was a bigamist and maybe had abandoned his daughters. My mama was crippled in a hospital bed.

Strangely, though, I didn't feel lost or terribly frightened. Maybe things were too bad for that. Or maybe the plates had shifted, but I was still standing, just in a slightly different place. Maybe more than slightly different. But standing.

I looked around the ugly little room. George was crawling across the floor looking for food. The old swag lamp over the table cast his shadow at the foot of the wall.

"Go get 'em, George," I said.

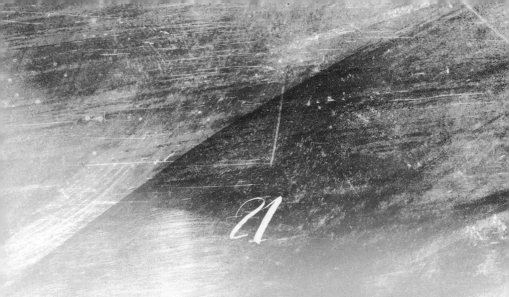

The next day, Rob took us down to see Mama during visiting hours. She was out of intensive care. She still looked like hell, but she perked up when she saw us.

"How are you doing?" she asked, like she was pleading.

"We're doing fine. Everybody's helping us. What do you need?" was what we told her.

"I don't need anything except to know that you're all right," she said. She paused, then she said, "Have you told your father yet?"

"As to that," I said. "No."

"You'd better," she said.

"We can't," I said, and then I told her why.

She started crying.

"Mama, it's all right," Thalia said. "It'll all be all right."

Mama cried more.

When she finally stopped, it seemed like a good time to ask a few questions that had been on my mind since yesterday.

"Mama, when did it happen?" I said. "And when did you find out?"

"And are there any other children?" Thalia said.

Mama looked at Thalia and shook her head no. Then she took a deep breath.

"Oh . . . he said he met her about three years ago," Mama said. "Her name's Irene and she's Greek. Really Greek. She'd been living in Athens until a few weeks ago. Then he brought her over and told me he wanted a divorce."

"I thought it was your idea, Mama," I said.

"It sure as hell is now," Mama said.

"How long ago did he marry her?" I asked.

"I'm not sure," Mama said. "At least a year. But he didn't tell me when it happened. He just let me know that it was time for us separate for a while. Not divorce—separate. That's when I started looking for a place for us. He didn't tell me he was married to her until she was in this country."

Thalia wasn't saying anything. She was just sitting by our Mama, white-faced as a Greek tragedy mask.

"But why didn't you tell us?" I said.

"How do you feel now that you know?" Mama said.

"Ashamed," I said. "Which is really stupid. I didn't do anything wrong."

"No," Mama said. "But that's how it is when you're a kid. Something goes wrong in your family and you feel like it must be your fault. I was the same way when I was young."

"Were you ever going to tell us?" I said.

"Of course," Mama said. "But your father and I agreed—it was the last thing we agreed on—that we'd pretend we just couldn't stand each other anymore, and that's why we'd split up. Then you'd find out he remarried. Then when you were older, I'd tell you the truth. I thought if we couldn't give you a normal family, we could at least give you a normal divorce."

She wiped her eyes.

"I was an idiot. You can't keep a thing like that secret. But I wanted—I wanted it to be better for you. Better than this."

I could feel those tectonic plates grinding again, one of those aftershocks where the huge slabs of basalt are settling into their new relationship with each other.

"Speaking of feeling ashamed," I said. "I'm sorry I've been such a pain in the ass."

"Don't be," Mama said. "It's my fault. I should have told you both what was really going on." Then she laughed a very little. "See? I'm still taking the blame, just like when I was your age. It's a tough habit to break."

"Mama," Thalia announced. "I hate him and I don't ever want to see him again. Please don't make me."

Don't worry about that, kid, I thought. *The old man may have come to the same conclusion.* But what I said was, "We don't need to worry about that right now, Thalia. It's just the three of us."

"Don't worry," Mama said, closing her eyes. "God, I feel better. Thank you, Elektra."

I leaned over and kissed her. So did Thalia.

⁓

Visiting hours were over.

Thalia and I walked down the hall to the lobby hand-in-hand.

"How is she?" Rob asked.

"We're all a lot better, I think," I said.

When we got home, Boozer welcomed us—I'd forgotten we'd left him inside—and ran out into the night.

"Probably has a meeting to go to," Rob said. "He pretty much runs this place. Well, good night. You know where I am if you need me."

He left us alone on our deck.

"How are you feeling, kid?" I asked Thalia.

"I don't want to talk about it right now," Thalia said.

This was not the Thalia I knew. She always wanted to talk, about everything. I wondered if this was the start of a modern Greek tragedy: daughter avenges betrayed mother, chops father to bits with double-bladed bronze axe. Film at eleven. I wanted to calm her down a little if I could.

"Let's take a walk," I said.

We headed toward the sad park at the end of Bodega Street then walked past the tables until we were clear of the lights from Guadalupe Slough. To the north, San Francisco, Oakland, and all the other towns I didn't know yet were glowing against the low, gray sky. The water lapped and shone at our feet.

We just stood there for a while and took it all in.

After a long time, Thalia began to sing one of her old, old songs,

"There's a city by a bay
Where the morning skies are gray,
And the hills rise up to meet the evening star.
And that's where I want to go,
For I left it long ago,
And I've traveled far too long and far too far.

Oh, San Francisco, San Francisco,

You'll never know how much I've missed you,

San Francisco, San Francisco,

When will I come home?"

And for a moment I had the most amazing rush, and I felt like I was everywhere at once. Here, and on the beach outside Troy, and connecting earth and heaven and everything I was. Elektra the Greek, Elektra the Mississippi girl, Elektra the bestrider of tectonic plates, sister and daughter and child of the stars.

The moment passed, and I was just Elektra again. Just Elektra? Hell, I was superwoman. Whatever tomorrow brought, I would do what Odysseus did: deal with it.

I threw back my head and shouted "*Aera!*" as loudly as I could. It's the ancient Greek battle cry, and it literally means, "Light!" We'd shouted it at Marathon when we beat the Persians by charging uphill in full armor. Melina Mercouri shouted it in *Never on Sunday* when she found out her boyfriend was using her. I shouted it now.

"You are such a geek," Thalia said.

"That's *Greek*," I said. "And what does that make you?"

"*Aera!*" Thalia shouted.

"*Aera! Aera!*"

The next day, I thought again about money. I remembered that Mama had worked as a dishwasher for a few hours at Alix's. That meant Alix owed her something. I decided to go over and get it.

Thalia tagged along—no, she came along—and we got there just before the place opened up for lunch.

Mr. Gonzales was mopping the floor.

"We're not open yet," he said.

"You work here, too?" I said.

"What's it look like? A man likes to keep busy," he said.

"Besides, he owns a quarter interest," Maizie said. "Can't get rid of him."

"How's your mother?" Mr. Gonzales said.

"She's a little better, thanks," Thalia said. "We'll tell her you asked."

"Whatever," Mr. Gonzales shrugged and moved away.

"Is Alix here?" I asked.

"Where else would she be?" Maizie said. "Check the bar."

"They can't go into the bar, they're kids," Mr. Gonzales shouted.

"It's not a bar till we're open," Maizie said.

"That don't matter," Mr. Gonzales said.

We went into the bar.

It was the first time for either of us, and I've never seen another one like it. The whole back wall was a forest of elegantly carved redwood that swooped and scrolled and glowed a rich red-brown. There were mirrors at the back etched with scenes that were supposed be Greek gods and nymphs getting down with each other. ("Oh, cool. Very accurate," I whispered to Thalia. "It depends what you mean by accurate," Thalia said, with a blush.)

Below the authentic Greek mythology lessons, the bottles were racked in perfect rows, ready for duty. There were all shapes of glasses, shining like the stars, and a brass cash register the size of our late, lamented Volkswagen, covered in bas-relief vines.

Against the wall on our left was a podium and something that looked like a throne with teeth. This was an organ keyboard, the biggest one I'd ever seen. Around the ceiling ran tubes that connected to strange-looking objects.

And in the middle of this splendor, at an elegant red-wood table that must have been a hundred years old, sat Alix. I felt like I should curtsy.

"Hi," she said. "I'll bet you kids have come for your mama's money."

"You win," Thalia said.

"Got it right here," Alix said, and she counted out two hundred dollars.

"That much?" I said.

"Two nights' work," Alix said. "And it's not that much. This damn bay area is one of the most expensive places to live in the country. Wait'll you see how fast it goes."

"Don't spend it all in one place," Maizie said and cackled.

Neither Thalia nor I had any idea why that was supposed to be funny.

Mr. Gonzales came in, climbed up on the organ throne, and ran his fingers over the keys.

"It's out of tune," he said.

"Your ears are out of tune," Maizie said. "That thing's perfect."

In response, Mr. Gonzales made the organ tweet like a

bird, chime like distant temple bells, whistle like a ferryboat, and drum a rapid military *ratatatat*. The strange objects on the ceiling all rang, thumped, and tweeted together.

"Now that's what I call music," Maizie said.

Thalia clapped.

"What kind of organ is that?" I said.

"It's an old silent theater organ," Alix said. "Just before sound came in, they made about six of 'em. This one ended up in a theater in San Francisco. That was in 1926. In 1927, they released the first sound picture, and by 1929, this thing was sitting in a warehouse down here in San José. I picked it up cheap about 1960. Didn't really need it, but it's hard for me to resist a bargain."

"It's the neatest thing I've seen since we got here," Thalia said, staring up at the mechanical bird.

Mr. Gonzales made the mechanical bird sing again while he played some sugary old tune that almost drowned it out.

"You know 'Red Sails in the Sunset'?" Thalia said.

"*You* know 'Red Sails in the Sunset'?" Mr. Gonzales said.

"That kid knows all kinds of old junk," Maizie said. "More than you, I bet."

"Bet she doesn't know this one," Mr. Gonzales said, and played a few bars of—

"'My Sweetheart Down the Lane,'" Thalia said.

"No way," Mr. Gonzales said.

"Hah," Maizie said.

"Don't you remember the night we had that party to celebrate Rob calling off his suicide, and you came by with your bat?" Alix said. "Who do you think that was singing?"

"Her?" Mr. Gonzales said. "She's too young to sound that good."

"Hah," Maizie said again.

"Where did you learn to play the organ, Mr. Gonzales?" Thalia said.

"From my grandfather. He was the organist over at St. Joseph's Cathedral. Wanted me to take over for him. I did for a while, but when he died, I quit. This is the kind of stuff I like."

And he played something with a skylark in it that I knew was by Johnny Mercer.

"This stuff was still on the radio when I was a kid," Mr. Gonzales said. "Not like the crap they have now. My God."

Thalia climbed up beside him and started to sing along. Mr. Gonzales softened the organ so that Thalia's clear, sweet voice flew above it, and they finished together like sunset and starlight.

"Damn," Maizie said as though she were praying.

"I know what you're going to say, Maizie," Alix said. "The answer is no."

"Come on," Maizie said. "You have him come in every Friday and Saturday night to play that thing and every drunk who can't remember the words sings along. This would be something good."

"She can't be in here during open hours," Alix said. "This is a bar, not a recital hall."

Maizie scuttled over to Thalia and dragged her down off the organ. She took her over to the entrance to the bar, which had two beautiful naked statues standing in niches on either side.

"Help me, kid," Maizie said to Thalia.

I joined them and the three of us moved one of the beautiful redwood goddesses out of her niche. Then Maizie pushed Thalia into it.

"She's not in the bar now," she said. "Sing something."

Thalia sang,

> "'Neath Southern stars
> In low bars,
> They blew notes
> High as Mars,

And they say that's

How the blues began . . ."

The notes of the organ slid in beneath her words perfectly.

"That could be like our theme song," Maizie said.

"We don't need a theme song," Alix said. Then she sighed deeply. "Okay, here's the deal: You can't work here. But, if you were to come in every Friday and Saturday night and just start singing . . . I'd give you a hundred bucks under the table against tips. Anything over that, we split down the middle. Want to try it?"

"Thank you," Thalia said. "I'll be here."

"Wait a minute," I said. "We have to think about this. It's kind of—"

"It's kind of perfect," Thalia said. "What else can I do to get money?"

"We sure can't use her to wash dishes," Maizie said.

"Okay, but I have to come with her," I said.

"Sure, whatever," Maizie said. "Right, Alix?"

"I said we'd try it," Alix said.

Mr. Gonzales ran his fingers up and down the keys.

"Do you know 'Stars Fell on Alabama'?" he said to Thalia.

Of course she did.

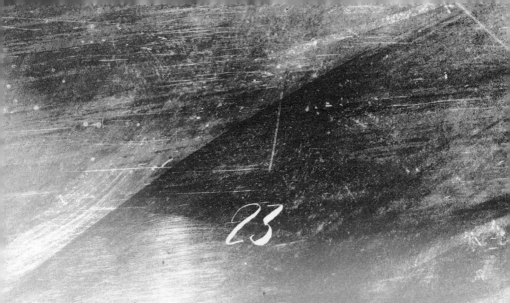

We decided to do for Mama what Emily Dickinson would have done. "Tell all the truth, but tell it slant." So when we went to see her later that day, we said that Thalia—and I—had a deal to help out over at Alix's on weekends and she was paying us under the table, and Mr. Gonzales would be there to help us and show us what to do. That's what we told her. Come on, was every word you ever spoke to your mother the Gospel truth?

She smiled and closed her eyes and said, "Maybe things are going to work out after all."

And they were working out, weren't they?

Then Rob took us home and we tried to figure out how to dress Thalia for her debut.

We'd left almost all our clothes in Mississippi. Neither of us had a dress with us, and there was no place in

Guadalupe Slough to buy one. Jeans and a T-shirt didn't seem quite the thing for a nightclub singer. What were we going to do?

"Let's go see if Erik's in the mood for a reference question," Thalia said.

The library was quiet the way it always was when we went in. An old lady was giving Ms. Torres money for her gas bill. Erik was dozing with his feet up on the desk and a cart of books beside him.

The lady took her receipt and headed out the door. Her steps as she left sounded loud as hobnail boots on the floor of an ancient tomb.

"Good-bye, Mrs. Silva," Erik said without opening his eyes. "See you next month."

"Hey, girls, how's your mother doing?" Ms. Torres said.

"You heard about her?" I said.

"Word has reached this institution that she is out of intensive care and resting well," Erik said. "Can you update us?"

"She's getting better every day," Thalia said. "Thank you for asking."

"How did you hear about it?" I asked.

"Rob told us," Ms. Torres said.

"Oh," I said.

I must not have sounded entirely happy about it, because Erik began to orate, which he did without either opening his eyes or taking his feet off the desk.

"Ms. Kamenides, you will have to expand your notions of privacy now that you are among us," he said. "We of the slough have only one, shared, existence. If life pricks you, do we not bleed? If life stomps you flat, does the mud from its big, dirty boots not stain us all? And you are privy to all our turbid ebbs and flows of human misery, as well. On the other hand, what happens in the slough, stays in the slough, slowly sinking down through the muck until it reaches the water table and washes out on the tide."

"We have a reference question," Thalia said. "A real one."

"I'm pretty busy," Erik said. "Can you come back Friday?"

"This is Friday," Thalia said.

Erik sighed, opened his eyes, and said. "Oh, well. How can I help you?"

We told him.

"Costume. 394.037," he said. "Sewing. 647.58. For that matter, popular music, 792.459. This question is an embarrassment of riches, actually. I thank you for asking it."

"She just needs something nice to wear for tonight," I said.

"Emergency calls, 9-1-1," Erik said. He swung his feet off the desk, picked up the old landline phone, and called someone.

"Good afternoon, Ms. Gonzales," he said. "This is the Guadalupe Branch Public Library calling. We are having a fashion emergency here and are hopeful that you can help. Right up your street, I think. Excellent. Thank you."

He hung up.

"A trained specialist will be with you shortly," he said. He put his feet back on the desk.

And a few minutes later, T'Pring walked in the door.

"Ms. Gonzales, the younger Ms. Kamenides is opening at Alix's tonight and needs something appropriate. What do you recommend?" Erik said.

"You're what?" T'Pring said.

When we had explained, she said, "Sounds like fun. Come on," and she led us over to her place.

Down in the hold of her boat were some big cardboard boxes, all alike, and all marked with notes that said things like BELLYDANCE: ALGERIAN, BELLYDANCE: PERSIAN, 1940S HATS, 1940S SHOES, and 1940S WOMEN'S SLACKS.

This was the first one she pulled out.

"You just keep old clothes lying around?" I said.

"I costume shows all over the South Bay," she said. "Belly dancing is seasonal. This gives me a way to make extra money sometimes. Now turn around," she said to Thalia. T'Pring looked Thalia up and down. "We're going to go for the 1940s career girl look. You're way too young for the evening gown thing. You'd look like a freak. People see you in pants and a jacket they'll think, 'Oh, okay. She's just a kid who's dressed up a little.' But they won't know they're thinking it. Take off your clothes."

T'Pring went to work cutting down a pair of high-waisted black slacks with wide flowing legs to fit my little sister. I helped out where I could. Then she found a white blouse that almost fit, and a little black jacket to go with it.

When she was done, Thalia was transformed. Into what, I couldn't say exactly, but she was definitely not what she had been.

"I think I got it," T'Pring said. "You don't look quite real, and you shouldn't. Kind of a World War II elf. What do you think?"

Thalia examined herself in a long mirror that T'Pring swung down from the ceiling.

"I look wonderful," she said.

"But what about shoes?" I said. "Tennis shoes don't exactly go with this outfit."

"I don't know. I don't have anything small enough for her feet," T'Pring said.

"What about ballet slippers?" Thalia said.

"What made you think of those?" I said.

"Well, they're simple and black and you brought some with you when we left Mississippi," Thalia said.

Which was true. I'd taken them with me, stuffed into the bottom of my one suitcase, because sometimes I wore them when I practiced belly dancing. With a coat of liquid black polish they might look all right in the dim light of Alix's dining room.

"Now what about you?" T'Pring said.

"Me? I'm not doing anything," I said.

"Yes, you are," T'Pring said. "You're keeping an eye on your sister while she sings to a bar full of people, some of whom are going to be stupid drunk. So we have to dress you, too. Jeans won't cut it."

Being almost grown, I was a lot easier to fit. T'Pring costumed me to look a lot like Thalia, but she updated the pantsuit to a much more recent decade and found some shoes to match. With a grim look to go with the outfit, I could probably outface any creep who tried to annoy my sister.

So we were good to go. And when I asked T'Pring how much we owed her, she told me and neither of us batted an eye. I liked that. Respect on both sides. I paid T'Pring out of mama's dishwashing wages.

When we went to Alix's that night, we went to the back door. I felt like a California show-business pro. Thalia, who actually was about to become a real California show-business pro, did not. She was just scared.

"You can get ready upstairs," Alix said when we came in. "We fixed up a place to change. Just like a real dressing room."

The place was a bathroom, but it said POWDER ROOM on the door. Along with the usual things a bathroom has, there was a dressing table, a small armoire, a potted palm, and a picture that made us look away.

"This seemed like such a good idea this morning," Thalia said as she changed into her singer's rig.

"It is," I said. "It's a great idea. All you have to do is sing the songs you've been singing since you were little."

"To a room full of strangers for money," she said.

"Well, if you don't like it, you can quit."

"What if I like it but I'm no good?"

"With any luck, they'll be too drunk to care."

"Oh, thanks."

"You're a Greek, and you're a siren," I said. "You can lure men to their deaths with your songs."

Thalia giggled.

"What am I supposed to do with a room full of dead men?"

"Just walk away innocently like 'Gee, I wonder how that happened?' while I go through their wallets," I said.

I put on my chaperone's uniform, and we were ready.

When we went downstairs, we passed Mr. Gonzales. He looked totally cool in a linen jacket and a cravat.

"This isn't me," he said. "T'Pring made me do it."

"Yeah, well she did the right thing," Maizie said as she came into the kitchen from the dining room. "Usually you look like a bum who wandered in and sat down at that organ to see what it was."

Mr. Gonzales ignored her.

"You ever use a mike before?" he asked Thalia.

"Nope," she said.

"Well you're using one tonight," he said. "Between me

and the customers, it's the only way you'll ever get heard. But it's a good one. We'll get a level on you, hang it around your neck, and you can forget about it. Right?"

Thalia reached out and squeezed his hand.

"You'll do fine, *m'hija*," he said. "Just remember who you're singing to. Me. Okay?"

Thalia nodded.

Once she had been miked, we went into the restaurant and Thalia took her place in the niche at the edge of the bar. I took a chair from one of the tables and sat nearby, trying my best to look fierce.

From what I could see, the customers were kind of a mixed bag. Some were young techie types with scraggly beards and jackets over their T-shirts sharing craft brews and ports. Some were older guys in suits who had women with them. The clothes, the drinks, and the people all looked expensive.

Mr. Gonzales came downstairs in his beautiful jacket. He smiled at me.

"Good scowl," he said.

"You know, this place doesn't make sense," I said. "Everything else in the slough is so down-home by comparison."

"Ah, there used to be places like this all around the bay," he said. "Places that didn't have what you might call 'too much law enforcement.' Where people came to get up to what they couldn't get up to closer to home. Joints like this made money. And they spent it on what you see. They're all gone now, except this one. And it's gone respectable."

He shook his head.

"Ah well," he said. "Better limber up."

He walked into the bar, climbed to his seat at the organ, and ran his fingers over the keys. Then he began playing, and Thalia, looking into the bar in his direction, started to sing.

Nobody noticed her until the end of her second song, which went up on a high C and dropped. Then heads turned her way. A few people stopped talking. A couple of them clapped a little. Thalia nodded slightly and waited for Mr. Gonzales.

He played three notes. That was enough for Thalia to recognize the tune, and she smiled. Once again, she started to sing.

By the end of their set, the big huge brandy snifter next to Mr. Gonzales's throne was full of bills. So was the one resting in the arm of the redwood goddess, which Alix had put there for Thalia. And most of them weren't ones. I tried not to look happy. My job was to glare.

But people will talk.

"Hey, kid, that's a great voice you have."

"Do you take lessons?"

"Will you be here next week?"

And, "How old are you?"

When Mr. Gonzales came back from his fifteen-minute break, Thalia was smiling. And she was ready to talk back.

"I want to thank y'all for coming to Alix's tonight," she said. "And I hope you like the music. Y'all can probably tell from the way I talk that I am not from around here. But people here in the slough have made us feel right at home. My mama and sister and me—that's my sister, Elektra, over there—"

I shrugged slightly and tried to look like a hitman, or at least a hitman-in-training.

". . . well, we're real glad to be here," Thalia went on. "And we hope you'll all come back on Friday and Saturday nights as often as you can for the music. Mr. Gonzales—up there at the organ—and I, we both love the old songs so much. We hope you do, too. And this is one of my favorites."

She lifted her little face toward the ceiling, pushed one foot forward, and threw back her arms.

"'Neath Southern stars

In low bars,

They blew notes

High as Mars,

And they say that's

How the blues began . . ."

No one spoke. Everyone listened. And when she was done, they took the roof off the place with their applause.

That little scoundrel was a siren, all right.

At midnight, Thalia bowed for the last time and disappeared upstairs. I followed her.

"Did I do good?" she asked, shucking out of her singing suit. "It seemed like a lot of people were putting money in that big glass thing."

"You flubbed two lyrics and your voice broke on one high note, but yeah. You did well," I said.

"I should have practiced more," Thalia said. "But I didn't want to wear out my voice. I'll do better tomorrow."

Maizie barged in without knocking. She was holding the big brandy snifter in front of her like a Cretan woman bearing a libation to her goddess.

"Let's settle up," she said.

We began by dividing the money into piles. We had a very high stack of ones, a pretty high stack of fives, one almost as high of tens, a cute little sheaf of twenties, and one lonely hundred dollar bill all by itself.

"A hundred dollars?" Thalia breathed.

"Well, hell, a lot of the guys in here are so stinking rich a hundred is chump change to them," Maizie said. "But, hey, let 'em show off if they want to. Good going, kid, good going."

When we'd split the money, Maizie and the Kamenides girls each had more than two hundred dollars.

"Wait'll I show this to Alix," Maizie said. "She'll plotz."

"She'll what?" I said.

"Fall over," Maizie said. "Faint. Don't you know anything?"

"I know you're a wonderful person," I said. "You made this happen."

"Fuck that," Maizie said and left.

Thalia sat down at the dressing table and looked at the stack of money that remained.

"I made that, didn't I?" she said. "I earned almost four hundred dollars today. And I work again tomorrow night."

The next day, we went to the Mercado and stocked up on supplies. It felt powerful to pay cash for everything we needed and to have money left over and know that there was more to come. But two things were worrying me. One was easy to fix—I just had to find Ralph and give him back what was left of his money. The other was to repay him for the spent part, and that would be harder. I wasn't going to use the money Thalia made singing. I didn't want her asking why I needed it.

Besides, lying to Ralph hadn't been one of my finest moments, and, unlike Odysseus, I was no longer trying to get home. This place was where I was. I had to act like I belonged here.

But first thing's first: it was time for morning visiting hours, and Rob was there to drive us to the hospital.

This time, Mama let him see her. Her face was still bruised, but the worst was beginning to fade, and some of the swelling was gone.

"They've given me a prognosis," she told us. "They say I can probably go home in another eight or nine days."

"That's wonderful," we said, as though it was wonderful that she would be here so long.

"We're already planning your coming-home party," Rob said, which was news to me.

"I'll still be in casts for months," she said. "I don't think I'll be up for any parties." She sighed. "I feel so damned useless."

"You're not useless, Mama," Thalia said. "You're sick."

"Chill, Mama," I said. "Things are flowing along pretty well."

"And, by the way, I've been in touch with Cleburne College," Rob said. "I finally got through to the department chair yesterday. He wasn't anxious to talk to me, but he did tell me where his former Greek tragedy professor is going to turn up next. Turns out a school in New Jersey had a spot for him. As soon as he gets there, I'll remind him he's still got responsibilities."

"It's so nice of you," Mama said. "But—"

"It's kind of fun to throw my weight around again," Rob said. "I hadn't realized I'd been missing it."

"Would you ever go back to being an attorney full-time?" Thalia said.

"And give up all this?" Rob grinned.

"How is your writing coming?" Mama asked.

"Been reading a lot. Trying to write something as good as what I read. Not making it. Same old, same old," Rob said.

"When I do get home, I'd love it if you'd come over and read me some of it," Mama said.

Rob blushed. Yes, he did.

"And maybe you could read me some of your work," he said.

"Well, something to look forward to to speed my healing," Mama said.

Thalia changed the subject to Mama's experience in the hospital. Mama held forth on the quality of the blankets (thin), the nature videos over her bed that were supposed to calm her (they helped), and the little unidentifiable squares of sweetness that were desserts (they could not be made from real food).

When visiting hours were over, we went back to the slough. Boozer was hanging out by the door when we got home. He and Thalia took off for a walk up the bike path.

I went looking for Ralph.

He wasn't home. His strange, crude statue stood guard over his place, just about as scary-looking as ever.

Well, shoot, I couldn't give him back his money if he wasn't home. Then, as I turned to go, I saw him lying in the mud and reeds a few yards away.

"Ralph, are you okay?" I said, running toward him.

He rolled over when he heard me coming and snatched up a rifle.

"No," I shouted. "It's just me."

"Advance and be recognized," he shouted back.

"Put that thing down first," I said. "I don't care if it doesn't shoot."

"Advance and be recognized," Ralph said.

"It's Elektra Kamenides, damn it," I said. "The one who owes you money?"

"Okay," Ralph said. "Come on ahead." He put the rifle down beside him.

"What are you doing out here?" I said.

"Reconnaissance," he said.

"But you live there."

"Yeah, but you never know."

"Ralph, I didn't go on my trip," I said. "I came to pay back some of what I owe you."

Ralph looked awful, even by Ralph standards. His old green jacket was covered with mud, and so was he. It was matted in his hair and beard and ground into his skin. He looked like Odysseus after a shipwreck.

It occurred to me to ask him when he'd eaten last.

Ralph smiled and pulled out three mashed candy bars from his pocket. A few empty wrappers fell out when he did it.

"I got plenty," he said.

I sniffed him.

"When was the last time you had a bath?"

"It was a while ago," he said. "Before they came again."

"The ones you're on guard against?"

"I heard them moving around last night," he said. "That's why I'm out here."

I sniffed again. Candy bars. Dirt. Body odor. And the look in his eyes sang of loneliness. For the first time I wondered why his friends in the slough let him live like this. Why couldn't they see what was in front of them?

"Have you got any other clothes?"

"I have lots of stuff," Ralph said. "But it's in there."

"Well, let's go in and get you some," I said. "We're going to get you cleaned up."

"I can't go in there," Ralph said. "They might still be around."

"Well, I'm going in," I said. "You can wait here if you want to."

Ralph looked worried.

"I'll cover you," he said.

"I'll cover myself," I said, picking up his useless old weapon.

"Bring back another one for me," he said.

"We won't need them where we're going," I said.

His boat was a sty, and it smelled so bad I wanted to turn around and get out into the open air again. His extra clothes were things he had already worn, left around everywhere. Candy bar wrappers and empty bags of chips joined them. One or two naked lightbulbs stuck out from odd corners, and a rusty sink sat full of everything but dishes. I wasn't sure where he slept, but it might have been on a worn bench by the galley. Or not.

I found a big plastic shopping bag and stuffed some of the clothes into it as quickly as I could. When I had loaded the bag with jeans, shirts, and parts of old uniforms, I went back out and found Ralph. He had moved a few feet to the right.

"Better recon from here," he explained.

"Mission accomplished," I said. "Come with me."

"Where are we going?"

"My place."

"Why?"

"To feed you and get you cleaned up."

"Oh. Why are we doing that?"

"I still owe you money, remember?"

"Oh, yeah," Ralph said.

When we reached our place, Thalia and Boozer were having another lovefest on the deck.

"Take these to the laundromat. Go. It's an emergency," I said, handing my sister the bag.

"Okay," Thalia said, taking in the situation. She went and got the laundry soap. "Back ASAP. Hi, Ralph."

Off she went with Boozer.

I took Ralph in, smell and all, and pointed him into the bathroom. "There's everything you need in there," I said. "Soap, shampoo, a bag of those little pink razors. Don't come out until you've used up at least half of what's in there. Meanwhile, I'm going to figure out what to cook. Right?"

"Right," Ralph said, and he disappeared into the bathroom. I heard the water start. I heard splashing. Then I heard occasional yells and curses. I was pretty sure those were the sounds of Ralph trying to shave with little pink throwaway razors.

Figuring out what to feed him was pretty easy. There aren't that many things that I know how to cook. And how far wrong can you go with hamburgers? By the time I heard the water turn off, I had two huge ones stacked with cheese and every green thing I could find waiting for him in our little oven.

But there was a problem. Ralph could not put on his old clothes again. That would defeat the whole purpose of the last half hour.

"Don't come out yet," I shouted through the door. "I'll be right back."

I dashed over to Rob's boat. He was sitting on the bow, watching seagulls with a pad of paper on his knees.

"Give me some clothes," I said.

"Why do you want my clothes?" Rob said.

"I am cleaning Ralph," I said. "And you, sir, are going to give me something for him to wear right now."

"Okay," Rob shrugged. "Come on in and get what you need."

I'd never seen Rob in anything but jeans and T-shirts, so I was surprised to find that he had all kinds of things in his chest, even a couple of out-of-date suits. I selected a cotton shirt with buttons and a pair of sweatpants with an elastic waistband. These seemed to be a bit larger than Rob's other clothes and they'd fit Ralph better. I grabbed some tube socks and cotton underwear to go with them.

"You'll get these back washed," I said.

"Cool," Rob said.

I wanted to ask him why he and the others on the slough hadn't taken better care of Ralph. But there was no time for that now. I went home.

"Okay, Ralph, you can get dressed," I said. I handed the clothes in through the door, keeping my head turned away.

In a minute, Ralph was out, looking clean, smelling clean. His long wet hair hung down like the curls on a Greek warrior. An old, scarred Greek warrior.

I sat him down and brought him the food. He devoured it.

"More?" I said.

"Mm-hm!" he said through a mouthful of hamburger.

I made him a plate of cold stuff this time. He inhaled that.

What I was going to say next felt like I was crossing a river I wasn't sure I wanted to cross. How much of a commitment did I want to make to him? But I couldn't not say it.

"Ralph, I owe you some money, and the only way I have to pay you back right now is to work. The money I owe you is going to have to wait a little. But I don't want to wait. So what we're going to do is this: You and Thalia and I are going to clean out your place. Then we are going to set up a schedule of times for you to eat real food and things like that. Okay?"

He looked puzzled.

"Why do you want to do all that?" he said.

"Because no one else is doing it, I guess."

"I get pretty crazy sometimes."

"Well why can't you be crazy and clean and well-fed?"

"I'm pretty busy."

I took a scrap of paper and wrote *Elektra and Thalia 2 PM Sunday.*

"This is your appointment," I said. "We are coming over tomorrow to clean your place. You will also eat dinner with us. You will not go off on a mission or anything else. Do you understand?" Then I said, "That's an order."

"It is?"

"You heard me."

Ralph took the paper and stuffed it in his pocket.

George came into the kitchen looking for his own lunch.

"Hey, George," Ralph said. "Good to see you, man."

He picked up George and began to play with him. I couldn't tell if George was happy to see Ralph or not, but at least he didn't bite him, and Ralph let George crawl all over him until Thalia came back with a pile of fresh, folded laundry.

Ralph disappeared into the bathroom. When he came out again, Ralph looked like Ralph, but he seemed changed. He kept brushing his hands softly over his clothes. And when he spoke, his voice was softer than I'd ever heard it before.

"You want to clean my place?" he said.

"Sunday at two," I said.

"You want to clean my place?" he said again.

"Yes."

"Guess I'd better get it straightened up then, or we'll never get done," he said. "Guess I'd better go. Thanks."

He took the rest of his clothes and headed to the door. "I'll go with you," I said. "Thalia, I'll be back in a few minutes."

"You'd better be," Thalia said. "Visiting hours."

When we got to his place, I handed him what was left of his money.

"Here you go," I said. "I forgot to give it to you earlier."

He took it without saying anything and folded it carefully and put it in his shirt pocket.

"You're going to come Sunday and clean my place?" he asked.

"Yes," I said.

He nodded and went inside his fence. I left him in his yard, standing in front of his statue. I wasn't sure, but I think he was talking to her.

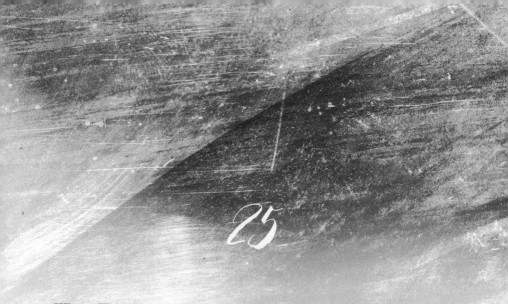

When Thalia and I got to Alix's that night, Carlos was waiting for us. He was dressed in a tux and a pair of dark glasses hung from his collar.

"Hey," he said. "I'm sorry I haven't been to see you. I've been up in Berkeley helping some friends with an art installation. I only heard about your mom today. How's she doing?"

"She's doing well, considering," I said. "Thank you for asking."

"You look nice," Thalia said. "Are you going somewhere?"

"Here," Carlos said. "I'm your sister's backup."

"Oh? Says who?" I crossed my arms and stuck up my chin.

"The *abuelito* himself," Carlos said. "He told me when I got back that Alix wanted me to help out. So I rented the tux and here I am."

"Well, that's very nice of them and you," I said. "But I don't think we need you. I did all right last night by myself."

"Watch," Carlos said. He put on the shades and loomed over us. His smile disappeared and a grim line replaced it.

I slipped my own glasses on and glared back at him.

We stood there eye-to-eye for a minute until Thalia said, "Well, I'm terrified. Excuse me while I go change."

"Seriously," I said. "I don't think we need you."

Carlos took off his glasses.

"Neither do I," he said. "But I want to do something to help. I won't stick around if you don't want me. But I'd rather stay. Can I?"

"Okay," I said. "Just stay out of my way if I have to resort to any rough stuff."

"Promise," Carlos said.

I started upstairs to go and change.

"You really do look kind of formidable," I said.

"Learning that look saved me from getting beaten up a lot in middle school."

The crowd at Alix's that night was bigger and noisier than the night before. But Rob, Ralph, Carlos, and T'Pring came in early and snagged a table down front, and that helped Thalia feel a little braver. Once again, the drinkers fell silent as Thalia and Mr. Gonzales raised the ghosts of songs long dead and poured their hearts into them.

I didn't exactly like having Carlos there. I thought it said something about what Alix thought of my ability to take care of my sister. But it was kind of fun to stand shoulder-to-shoulder with him, looking like a couple of secret service agents. While Thalia snag and sang, without forgetting a word or hitting a false note.

And our share of the take at the end of the night was close to five hundred dollars.

"Ah cain't hardly believe it nohow," Thalia said in her thickest fake Southern accent. She was so amazed at herself she had to make a joke of it.

"Well, honeychile, y'all just keep it up," Maizie said. "'Cause the bar receipts are even better than this. Listenin' to y'all seems to make the customers damn thirsty."

Neither of us bothered to explain that y'all is properly plural and a useful distinction of speech that Yankees would do well to learn and adopt. Wonderful, lovely Maizie had brought us to this night, and she could talk any way she wanted to.

Carlos, Rob, Ralph, and Mr. Gonzales were there to walk us home, which was nice, given all the cash Thalia was carrying. We were going to have to get a bank account or a safe deposit box or something.

We all said good night, and Ralph promised to take the first watch.

"You know, you still haven't seen my studio," Carlos said, turning back. "If you want to come by tomorrow, I'll be up there."

"Tomorrow's no good," I said. "I've got to visit my mother and I promised Ralph I'd help clean his place."

"Like I said, let me know how I can help," Carlos said. He waved and sauntered down the street elegant and out of place as a cheetah in his tuxedo.

ᯓ

I showed Thalia my tape-the-money-under-the-drawer trick, as if it were something I'd just thought of. Then we went to bed.

"I've been thinking about Mama," Thalia said as we lay close together enjoying the darkness. "We have to tell her, but I don't want to. But we have to, don't we?"

"The question is, will she worry more thinking we don't have any money, or will she worry more knowing we have some, but we're making it working for tips in a bar," I said. "I've been trying to work that one out myself."

"What would you rather worry about?" Thalia said.

"For me that's easy," I said. "I'd rather worry about you singing in a repurposed brothel. That's a lot better than worrying about no money. But I'm not your mother."

"Problem is, the longer we don't tell her, the madder she's going to be when she finds out," Thalia said

"I'm pretty sure she'd never forgive us," I said.

"I'm pretty sure she'd kill us," Thalia said.

"Yep," I said. "So it looks like we have to tell her the truth."

"Well, shoot," Thalia said. "Who's going to do it?"

"I am," I said. "I'm older."

"Good. Thanks," Thalia said.

꙳

When we went to see Mama the next morning, she looked a little better. Thalia and I were still sleepy from our night of hanging out in bars and talking in bed. And Mama noticed.

"You guys look like you stayed up too late," she said.

I shrugged.

"I didn't sleep much either," Mama said. "Apart from the fact that they wake me up every two hours to ask if I'm sleeping—I spend a lot of time thinking about things. Money, mostly."

This seemed like the time to mention Thalia's job.

"We're doing okay, Mama," I said. Then I took a deep breath. "The fact is, Thalia made about a thousand dollars this weekend."

"Doing what?" Mama gasped.

I told her.

"Oh, my God, she's doing *what*?" Mama said. "And you let her?"

"Thalia's good," I said. "And it's not like it sounds. Everyone takes care of us. Alix, and Maizie, and Mr. Gonzales, and everybody we know."

"I don't care. You've got to be breaking some kind of laws," Mama said. "Child labor or something. And even if you're not, Thalia's just too young. I can't believe Rob let you do this."

"Rob didn't have anything to do with it," I said.

"Oh my God, oh my God," Mama said. "I've got to get out of here. I've got to get home. You two are running wild." She reached over and grabbed the bell button with her good arm. "I'm checking out," she said.

But Thalia took the bell away from her.

"Stop it, Mama," she said.

Mama looked shocked. So did I.

"What did you just do?" Mama said.

"Mama, listen," Thalia said. "I know you're worried about what I'm doing. But there's nothing wrong with it. Some good people are helping us to stay in our place—which is the only place we've got right now—and to pay our own way. I know that makes you feel bad, like you shouldn't even be in here; but, Mama, where else can you be right now? You're sick. If you were well, you'd do anything for us, but you're not, so let us do this for you. You're always talking about dwelling in possibility. Well, this is the only possibility we've got right now. Try to be happy about it. And if you can't be happy, at least don't be ashamed. And don't worry."

Mama started to tear up.

"If I'd just turned right instead of left like I was supposed to, none of this would be happening," she said.

"That's right," Thalia said. "But then you'd never have let me sing at Alix's, and they'd never have asked me to anyway. And it's the best thing I can do to help. I know things are all messed up right now, but they're going to get better. Please, Mama. Don't worry so much about us."

Damn, my little sister was doing the job I was supposed to do, and she was doing it better. She was growing up fast, the little sneak.

Mama cried some more, and Thalia and I took turns hugging her until she stopped.

"Well, anyway," she said, wiping her eyes. "You've given me a hell of a lot of incentive to get well and get out of here."

"Just get well," we told her. And, "We'll see you tonight."

So that was one hill climbed, or river crossed, or something, and even though Mama wasn't happy about what we were doing, she wasn't angry, and we didn't have to lie to her and we were going to go on doing it. So that was better.

Rob took us home.

When we got there, I loaded cleaning things into a cardboard box and started off for Ralph's.

"You know what, we owe Rob a cleaning, too," Thalia said.

"We'll just have to catch up" I said. "We have a Ralph emergency to deal with first."

"You know, this is just like the Augean Stables," Thalia chirped as we started to clean Ralph's place. "If we could just run that little river through here, we'd be done in no time."

The Augean Stables hadn't been cleaned for twelve years. Cleaning them out was one of the impossible labors of Hercules, and running a river through them was how he accomplished it. And yes, the little Guadalupe River did trickle into the bay not far from here, but it clearly wasn't up to the job of cleaning out Ralph's boat, even if Hercules had been available to divert it.

And I am certain the Augean Stables didn't have tarantulas running around them. After I met the fifth one, I said, "Ralph, please, please, please put your tarantulas away, would you please?"

Which he did. He stuffed them all into a huge empty jar that said SUN TEA on it, and they spent the rest of the afternoon crawling over each other trying to get out.

Finally, King Augeas had wanted his stables cleaned. Ralph was less certain about his boat.

"I need that," "I use that," "I want to keep that," was what he kept saying about almost every broken radio, worn-out towel, and used-up battery.

But Thalia turned out to be a match for him.

"Ralph, these batteries need to be recycled. Now what you can do right now is put tape over their ends so we can do that." And Ralph would go look for some tape and get to work.

"Ralph, seventeen broken radios are too many for one boat. You just need one for each room. You've got two rooms, so pick the two best ones and get rid of the others," she said.

"How do I know which two to keep?" Ralph asked.

"This one and this one," Thalia said. "They go with the place. Now take the others outside and pile them up, please."

And Ralph did.

There was one job I had reserved for myself. A thing so horrible that it would, if I succeeded, qualify me for entry into the pantheon of Greek heroes. I was going to deep clean Ralph's bathroom. Nobody was going to call Elektra Kaminedes a coward. I set my jaw and headed in, taking with me everything that scrubbed, polished, cleansed, and killed mold.

Of course, what I am calling the bathroom was more properly called the head, since it was on a boat. And since it was on a boat, it was tiny. I barely had room to stand, let alone work, but work I did, with my nose up against the walls and just above the floor. I cleaned everything in that damn place. Then I did it again.

When Thalia wanted to use it, I sent her back to our place. Nobody was going to interrupt me. If I stopped, I might never get started again. Every curve, every edge, every place where one thing joined another, I worked on while Thalia and Ralph took care of the rest of the purge.

What would Odysseus do if he discovered that his home, the only thing he cared about, no longer existed? That his wife and son didn't want him back? He'd never had to face that, but I did. And if he had, maybe he'd have cleaned the bathroom of a nice, crazy guy he'd lied to.

We didn't perform miracles that day. By the time we quit, we had only made a dent, and we had a mountain of cloth things to take to the laundromat on Monday. But Ralph could sit at his table if he wanted to, and there was nothing rotting in his refrigerator or his sink, and his last four checks from the Veterans' Administration, the only ones that could still be cashed, were taped to the refrigerator ready for the morning.

Hercules could not have done more. Not without a river.

But I wasn't finished. I still owed.

"Ralph, go take a shower and put on some clean clothes," I said. "Thalia, go get Rob away from his poems. We're going over to our place. I'm going to make Sunday dinner. Time to invite folks to share it."

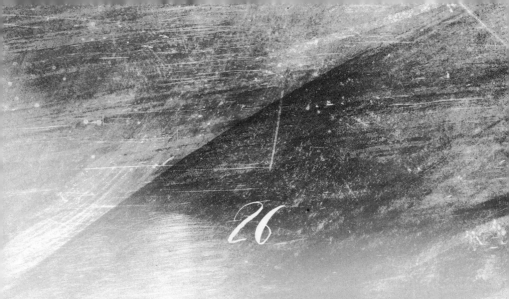

Rob looked amazed when he saw Ralph.

"Man, you look shiny new," he said.

"Yeah. I'm not, though," Ralph said. "Still me."

Dinner was chicken and rice and a sauce that Thalia and I whipped together by taking turns putting things in. Not the best ever, but it covered the rice all right, and the guys were happy as a couple of stray cats with fresh trash. Boozer showed up, of course, and George came out to say hello.

"I think he remembers me," Ralph said. "Hey, old buddy, how's the roach-eating life?"

When dinner was done, I thanked Ralph for coming, and the other three of us got in Rob's car. We still had time to see Mama before the end of visiting hours.

During the drive to the hospital, Rob was smirking and smiling and humming some earworm of a song.

"Did you have a good writing day?" I said.

"Not so much," he said. "But in another way it was a very good day. I'll tell you all about it when we get to the hospital."

When we got to the waiting room, Thalia took Rob by the hand and led him down to Mama's room. Mama perked up when she saw us.

"I'm starting to get really bored," she said. "I think that's a good sign."

"Indubitably," Rob said. "And the news I have should help you to get even better." He made a pointy little roof with his fingers the way people do when they're very pleased with themselves. "Guess, favorite clients, who's turned up?"

"From the fact that you're addressing us as clients, I guess it has to be Daddy," I said.

"She's sharp, the kid is sharp," Rob said. "He has fetched up at Kingston University, and he has just been congratulated on his new position and advised by Robert J. Schreiber, Esquire, that his real wife will be making some insurance claims. So your dear mother won't be set out at the curb with the recycling anytime soon."

"Oh," Mama said.

"How did you find him?" Thalia said.

"It wasn't hard," Rob said. "He isn't really trying to hide. Anyway, not from me. We have had a full and frank discussion of some of the distinctions between California and Mississippi divorce law, and events are now taking their course. Community property was a concept that he found surprising, but I managed to get his head around it. We'll be filing the papers next week."

"What community property?" Thalia said.

"Fifty-fifty split right down the middle, that's the basic principle," Rob said. "Of course it can get a lot more complicated. Which Professor Kamenides had better hope it doesn't."

Rob's chipperness got my back up. The thought that Daddy was back in our lives, willingly or not, was a fresh stab in my heart. I'd been able to push my pain away a little during the weekend with the weird excitement of Thalia going into show business, but this was Sunday night, and it was time to start hurting full-blast. So Rob had found Daddy, but Daddy hadn't told me where he was going. He'd talked to Rob but not to me. Somehow the fact that Rob had gotten him to promise to pay Mama's medical bills made him seem farther away than ever.

"Thank you for finding so much professional satisfaction in the breaking up of our family," I said.

I threw myself at Thalia and started to cry. So did she. Then Mama started and we all held each other. Rob just stood there not knowing what to do.

I waved him away, and he went out of the room.

When we had all calmed down a little, Mama said, "Well, that was cathartic, wasn't it?"

Thalia and I smiled at her weak joke—catharsis is supposed to come at the end of a day watching three tragedies in a row, the way the Athenians did. It's the release of all the fear and pity that has been built up. But I didn't feel released, just worn out.

Mama closed her eyes. I brushed away the tears she couldn't reach with her broken arm.

"Thank you, honey," she said. She drew a deep, shuddery breath and went on. "Listen, now. This is a hard thing for all of us. It's saying good-bye without really saying it. Because your father is always going to be a part of our lives. I was married to that man for twenty years. That's almost half my life. And you've known him every day since the sun first shone on you. He won't be gone. It'll never be the way it was, but he won't be gone. And if you want something to hope for, you can hang on to that. The future always gets here. And your future with him may be better than the past."

"If he wants a future with us so much, why hasn't he called or anything?" Thalia said.

"Because he's ashamed of himself," Mama said.

"Damn well should," I said.

"Well, he is," Mama said. "Now one of you'd better go get Rob."

I felt a little better toward him than I had, but I still shook my head.

"I'll do it," Thalia said. "I'm the one who likes stray dogs around here."

She led Rob back in, and he was different.

"Forgive me," he said. "I'd been psyching myself up for making that call. I thought it was going to be much worse than it was. But I have to say your dad took responsibility right away when I told him the situation. I've had much worse, believe me."

Mama nodded.

"Look," Rob said. "I'm not really much good at feelings. Most lawyers aren't. To get through law school you've got to be able to put your life on hold for three years and do nothing but study. And if you succeed at that, there's the bar exam. And then, if you pass that, what have you got? A chance to hang out with a bunch of other lawyers. And you'd be surprised how many of them hate the whole thing, but won't quit because that's where the money is. Blah, blah, blah. Sorry. For the last five years, I've been trying to turn myself into something else. A guy who can feel things, and write about them. But it's hard for me. So if I hurt your feelings just now, believe me, I'm sorry. But I'm just trying to help."

"We know," I said.

"We really do," Thalia said. "And, since we're talking about feelings, we know you like our mama, and we're trying to be happy about that."

Rob looked stunned, like Thalia had hit him upside the head with a bataka bat.

"Uh, well . . ." he said.

"But we're all going to have to give each other time," I said. "It's gonna take time for Mama to heal, and for us to heal, too."

"Girls, please shut up," Mama said.

"Absolutely," Rob said.

"Absolutely shut up, or absolutely we need time?" Thalia said.

"Both," Rob said. "Absolutely both. And it's getting late."

"Absolutely," Mama said.

"See you tomorrow," I said.

Rob was silent as we went down the hall.

He was silent when we walked out to the parking structure and got into the car. He was silent until we got onto the expressway that led back to the slough. Thalia and I waited.

"You blindsided me back there," he said as we stopped for a long red light. "I really wish you hadn't done that."

"Had to come up sooner or later," I said. "You two have been flirting since we got here."

Rob's breath out was as slow as the light.

"Listen," he said. "I've handled a lot of divorce cases. I've seen a lot of people go through what your mother is going through now. And practically all of them get a case of the PDCs at some point. So don't tease us. Especially don't tease your mother. You don't know what's really going on with her."

"PDCs?" I said.

"Pre-Divorce Crazies or Post-Divorce Crazies," Rob said. "Some people get both. When you're splitting up, you can find yourself getting really attracted to somebody you would never in a million years fall for any other time."

"You think Mama's got the PDCs for you?" Thalia said.

"No," Rob said. "And I don't want her to. I mean, anything between us, I'd want it to be realer than that. Now let's change the topic, please."

"Good idea," I said.

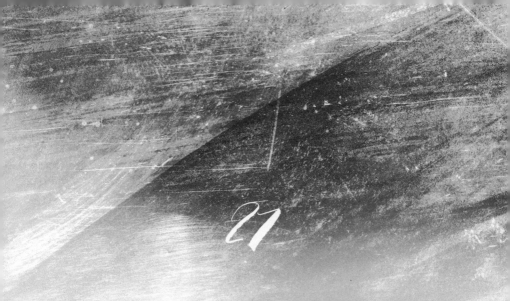

I saw Carlos around a few times during the week. He always repeated his offers of help, and that was nice, but what could anyone do that they weren't already doing?

We went to see Mama twice a day. In between we tried to find things to do.

We got library card applications and took them to Mama to sign. She signed them with her uninjured hand and cried because the awkward angle made her name a scrawl.

We started checking out books a hundred a day each. Boozer hung out with Thalia. We met a few more of the people who lived in the little houses that filled the blocks between the bay and the freeway.

Then, on Thursday, I ran into Carlos at the Mercado when I went to get milk. He was sweeping the floors with a huge push broom and humming one of Thalia's old songs.

"Hey," he said. "Tell your sister thanks for the earworm. That thing she sings about stars on Alabama keeps rattling round in my head and I don't even like it that much."

"Tell her yourself," I said. "You'll be at Alix's tomorrow night, won't you?"

"Sure," Carlos said. "Seems to be the only thing I can do."

I thought about how much he wanted to help us, and how little so far he'd been able to do. I thought maybe if I asked to see his studio as he'd offered that maybe he'd feel a little better.

So I said, "Is this a good time to see your temple of art?"

"Just let me get this aisle finished."

꩜

The roof of the Mercado was a cluster of sawhorses, workbenches, and tool chests. There was sawdust in low, broad heaps that the wind was starting to blow around. Amid all this stood three large pieces of wood that were on their way to becoming a bird, a dolphin, and a tree.

"This seems like a weird place to have a studio," I said. "What do you do when it rains?"

"Move the tools under cover," Carlos said. "The rest doesn't matter. This stuff's intended to be outdoors anyway."

"But why don't you find someplace with a roof?"

"I like it up here," Carlos said. "It's private, it's quiet, it's big. The light's always changing and that can change the way I see a piece when I'm working on it. Plus, the slough is home—you know? I like being up here where I can see all of it."

"I hear you," I said. "I had a home myself until quite recently."

"Do you like it here?" And in spite of the easy way he said it, I had a feeling there was a lot riding on my answer.

"Yeah," I said. "I like it quite a bit."

"Good," he said. "Because I don't know you very well, but it seems like you really belong here."

"Why do you think so?" I asked.

"You're your own person," Carlos said. "The slough can be a good place for people who aren't trying to be someone they're not."

"Thank you," I said. "Nobody's ever said anything like that to me before."

And then there was something else on the roof with us. Something that wanted us to draw together the way we had when we'd danced on Rob's boat. I could see Carlos felt it too. The wind was blowing hard and the afternoon light was turning gold as the sun headed west, and in a movie this would have been the moment for the first kiss.

But we stayed where we were, neither of us certain of the other, and the sun touched the edge of the evening clouds coming in from the sea.

"Well," I said. "I'd better get going."

"Thanks for coming up," Carlos said. "See you tomorrow night."

~⁀∽⁀

Friday night at Alix's, was another success, but not as big as the one on Saturday night, when Thalia kept nearly a thousand dollars after the split with Alix.

"If this keeps up, we can take care of Mama ourselves," she said when we'd counted the money.

"Aw, you can't count on customers, honey," Maizie said. "They come, they go."

"Well, I'm going to dwell in possibility," Thalia said.

"Dwell in possibility? That's a hot one," Maizie said. "Good way to get your ass burned."

"Yeah, maybe," Thalia said. "But right now, we've got no place else to dwell."

"You've got a point," Maizie conceded and cackled.

Thalia and I were busy now. We continued to visit Mama

twice a day, and Thalia had to rehearse. She also had primary duty for getting Ralph to the laundromat. I saw there was something decent to eat in his refrigerator. We both tried to keep an eye on him, as much as we could. He wouldn't always let us on his boat, and of course he went out most days and didn't come back till late, and once or twice he was gone overnight, but sooner or later he'd turn up, dragging his big, flat wagon. When he did, we fed him, reminded him to shower, and made sure he changed his clothes.

Boozer was more regular. He came by several times a day, sometimes to scrounge and sometimes just to check in. He usually spent the night.

Mama was told she could come home next Sunday. She'd still be in a wheelchair, and she'd need all kinds of help to get around, but we'd be together again.

Word got around.

Alix and Maizie showed up with an old porcelain basin, because, "You'll never get your mama into that shower. With this you can wash her down no problem."

"That's an antique. We want it back," Maizie added.

And Rob kept pushing the ugly divorce things along. They went slowly, but at least they were going, sort of like a rat through a boa constrictor.

Then Ralph brought a wheelchair.

"Been looking for one of these," he said. "Needs some work, though."

Indeed it did. What Ralph had brought us was a rust-spotted frame and a pair of wheels with missing spokes. There were no handgrips, and only one brake. At least that was on the side of Mama's unbroken arm.

But Ralph's find had one huge virtue: it was free. And as Thalia and I looked at it, we had an idea that it might be made to work. And we knew who could help us with it.

"Go get Carlos," I told Thalia. "Tell him there's something he can do to help."

For the next few days, the three of us got (some of) the rust off and squirted lubricant onto the axles. Then we spray painted it gold. We got some old velvet curtain material from T'Pring and made a seat and back for the thing. We duct-taped the handles, and Carlos invented a sling for Mama's leg out of some sticks and the rest of the curtains. When this was all done, we had a party and Antonio showed us how to make his special flags. But instead of flags, we all made letters. When we sewed them on the next day, they spelled out POSSIBILITY.

Carlos and Antonio showed up the next day to reinforce

the ramp. By the time they were done, it looked more permanent than the home it was attached to.

And while Thalia and I were standing there admiring their work, T'Pring came along and said, "What's your mom's favorite color?"

"Provençal blue," I said.

"Paint it, you two," she said.

And of course, they did. And it was beautiful.

"God, artists are wonderful," Thalia said when we were all standing around admiring the drying paint.

"They have their points," T'Pring said.

"We're sort of like handymen with big imaginations," Carlos said.

And big hearts, I thought. *Y'all in particular.*

⁓

The day after that, my phone buzzed. I was at the library checking out my one hundred books, so I left the stacks on Erik's desk and went outside to take it.

I hadn't had a call since I left Mississippi—okay, a few robots had phoned to tell me about great investment opportunities, but that had been the extent of my online social life. So I was pretty curious when I said "Hello?"

"Elektra, it's your father."

I didn't know what to say. I became a theater of emotions in one second flat; joy, anger, curiosity, and contempt were all trying to grab the mike from each other.

"Can you talk?" Daddy said.

I nodded.

"Elektra, can you—"

"Yeah," I said.

"I suppose I haven't done a very good job of keeping in touch."

There were so many answers to that, and I couldn't decide which one to use.

"I've been—I've been remiss," Daddy went on. "I'm sorry I haven't done a better job—I mean, I need to do more. To keep in contact during this difficult time—"

"Why haven't you called Thalia?" I asked.

"We've always been closer, you and I," Daddy said. "Thalia is more your mother's than mine."

"Thalia's her own," I said.

"Elektra, please just listen," Daddy said. "This is very hard for me."

"Not too easy for me, either," I said.

"Please just listen," Daddy said again. "Thalia—damn it, I mean Elektra—there are things that happen in life that we can't control. And when those happen, everything gets upset for a while. I know that you and your sister and your mother must hate me now. I won't blame you for that. I only want you to understand that it's as hard for me right now as it is for you. And for Irene—"

"Irene, who's that?" I said. "Your other one?"

I couldn't say "wife." My tongue wouldn't let me.

"Yes. And she's very upset about the way things are now. In fact, she wanted me to make this call. She says we have to start mending."

"Oh. So it wasn't your idea," I said.

"Elektra, I love you," Daddy said.

"I love you, too, Daddy," I said. "But you're a no-good bastard and I don't want to talk to you right now. I don't want to talk to you until it's your idea, and you want to talk about something besides yourself. Thanks for calling. Love you. Good-bye."

And I hung up.

It hadn't been closure, whatever that's supposed to be. It hadn't been the future Mama had talked about. And it sure hadn't helped either of us. It was too soon for any of that. I wasn't ready for that, and neither was Daddy, for sure. I supposed the day would come when we might start to mend, but there was no way to push it. Catharsis only comes at the end of the tragedy. Never in the middle.

The day came for Mama to come home. Since she'd need the entire back seat of Rob's car, only Thalia or I could go along—not both. We flipped a coin, and I won.

Mama was ready when Rob and I showed up. She was up in a hospital wheelchair and had a plastic bag with what few things she'd kept with her sitting on her lap.

"Let's get out of here," she said. "I want to go water skiing."

An aide pushed her down the hall, onto the elevator, and down to the lobby while the three of us nattered away.

We carefully got Mama out of the chair and into Rob's back seat with her injured leg lying along it and her back against the far door.

"Are you comfortable?" I asked.

"Hell, no, but who cares?" Mama said. "My God, there are still colors in the world. Who knew?"

Rob drove home extra carefully, which made our trip to the slough even longer than usual. And he stopped for coffee because Mama hadn't had a cup she liked since her crash. So it was late afternoon before we got home.

Thalia, Alix, Maizie, Antonio, Carlos, Mr. Gonzales, T'Pring, Ralph, and Boozer were all sitting on Rob's deck when we drove up. Antonio's flags were flying over them.

Thalia jumped up and ran over to our place and got the wheelchair.

When she saw it, Mama said, "I don't know whether to laugh or cry."

"Then you're dwelling in possibility," I said. "Congratulations, you made it."

The three of us got Mama into the chair. Rob pushed her over to his boat.

"I hope you're ready for a party," he said. "Even if you only stay for a little while. We're all glad you're back. See? Even Mr. Gonzales is here."

"Without his bat," Mama said. "I'm flattered. Well, I didn't think I wanted a party, but after what feels like half a life in a hospital bed, maybe I need one. Anyway, it's here, so let's do it."

Somehow we got her up onto the deck, and the party started. Mama was the center of everything until she said she was tired and asked to be taken home. Then we managed to lower her down again and ran her back to our place.

She loved her blue ramp. And Thalia and I were mighty pleased with her reaction to the trailer.

"It's all clean," she said. "It's so clean. Even the roaches look clean."

"What roaches?" I said. "Are you implying George isn't doing his job?"

We helped her out of the wheelchair and onto the sofa. We stole a blanket and pillow off the bed and made her a cup of coffee to set her up proper.

When she was as comfortable as she was going to be, she tried to get us to go back to the party.

"Go on," she said. "I'll be fine. I'm home now."

"Mama, don't you get it? We want to be where you are," I said.

Mama closed her eyes and smiled.

But later, after Mama had fallen asleep, I did go out for a little. Not back to the party—I'd had enough of this one and there would always be another. So I just waved as I passed Rob's boat. I just wanted to be quiet and by myself for a little.

Here I was. I still hardly knew where I was, but this was it.

It was just past sunset, and Ralph's St. Barbara, the Muse of the Slough, was looking out to the bay, watching the lights of San Francisco and Oakland and all the towns around them. In ancient times, a thing like that might have been the guardian spirit of a sacred place. Places used to have guardian spirits—nothing you could see or touch, but a feeling that might come out in various ways. Guadalupe Slough sure had that all right.

Mama hadn't really pushed us out of our old lives; our old lives had fallen apart around us and Thalia and I hadn't known it. Mama could have played it safe, and she hadn't. She'd taken a flying leap and landed here. So far, dwelling in possibility wasn't paying off as she'd hoped. And I had lost all my old possibilities and didn't even know what new ones I wanted yet. But little old Thalia was blossoming like night-blooming jasmine, and she hadn't even been trying.

Maybe it was a little like the dervish dance. Because what you're really doing when you try to unite heaven and earth is fit yourself into the flow of the connection. Now that I knew my old life was gone, maybe the thing for me to do was not to try for a new one, but simply to let it come. WWOD? Not that, for sure. But Odysseus didn't have all the answers.

Neither did I. I didn't have any answers. But I knew I had possibility.

ACKNOWLEDGMENTS

I would like to thank Hilary Langhorst for providing photographs of Alviso as it was; Lance Morton, MSW, for his help in understanding Ralph's mental health problems; Dr. Bruce Davis, MD, for his insights into Helen's accident; and Eric Elliot, Carol Wolf, and my wife, JoAnn, for their feedback on the story as it progressed.

ABOUT THE AUTHOR

Douglas Rees grew up near various air force bases in California, Germany, and Massachusetts, which is the setting for his most popular work, *Vampire High*. Rees's first novel was *Lightning Time*, published in 1999. Since then, he has written picture books, a few short stories, and more novels. *Elektra's Adventures in Tragedy* is his fifteenth book published in hardcover. He writes: "Hard as it may be to believe, Guadalupe Slough is very close to being a real place. It was real once, before the unending spread of Silicon Valley's high-tech energy engulfed much of it. The cannery, the stores, houses on mounds, restaurants, and the string of boats were all there. I used to work sometimes at the little log library. Now it's gone, too. Elektra's story originates in an encounter I had with an English teacher who told me that when she was divorced and broke, she and her kids lived on one of the boats and gathered wild mustard for salads."

When he's not writing stories, he writes plays. Some of these have been produced in theaters from Oregon to Panama. "Writing a play is very different from writing a novel," he says. "Writing a novel is like hanging out on the playground with your friends. You can do all kinds of things until the bell rings. Writing a play is like fencing. You can't waste anything, and it all has to be to the point."

Doug works as a youth services librarian at the south end of San Francisco Bay, where he lives with his wife and two cats. His website is douglasrees.com.